# FEMALE—HANDLE WITH CARE

## Peter Chambers

## CHIVERS
### THORNDIKE

This Large Print edition is published by BBC Audiobooks Ltd, Bath, England and by Thorndike Press®, Waterville, Maine, USA.

Published in 2004 in the U.K. by arrangement with the author.

Published in 2004 in the U.S. by arrangement with Peter Chambers.

U.K. Hardcover  ISBN 0–7540–6960–5 (Chivers Large Print)
U.K. Softcover   ISBN 0–7540–6961–3 (Camden Large Print)
U.S. Softcover   ISBN 0–7862–6619–8 (Nightingale)

The text of this Large Print edition is unabridged.
Other aspects of the book may vary from the original edition.

Set in 16 pt. New Times Roman.

Printed in Great Britain on acid-free paper.

**British Library Cataloguing in Publication Data available**

**Library of Congress Control Number: 2004103446**

# FEMALE—HANDLE WITH CARE

# ONE

Abigail H. O'Hagan was the most exciting, exasperating and extraordinary female who ever walked into my office. What can you do with a woman who absolutely refuses to conform to any accepted pattern of behavior, whether it's business, social or—

Wait a minute. I'm not telling this right. It's not reasonable to expect people to understand if they come in half-way through the picture. The place to start is at the beginning.

So.

It began in my office.

I occupy two rooms on the third floor of a modern block near the seafront in Monkton City, Southern Cal. When there isn't any low cloud you can just catch a glimpse of what the tourist bureau calls the rolling blue Pacific. The legend on the outer door reads 'Mark Preston Investigations', and that's what I do for a crust. I've been doing it long enough now for people to feel they can trust me, and I get paid often enough to meet my heavy outgoings. These include the office rental, Florence Digby—I'll get back to her later, an expensive apartment over at Parkside, and half the town bookies. So far as Florence is concerned, my apologies if I express myself badly. What I should have said is that Florence

1

works for me. She is what you might call my confidential secretary, my accountant, filing clerk, records keeper and campaign manager. The campaign she manages has nothing to do with politics. It is her personal vendetta against my reluctance in the work area. My enemies will tell you that but for La Digby I would be insolvent within a week. There are always people like that around, ready to knock a man. Personally, I'm sure I could last out for maybe as long as ten days.

If Florence had been in her proper place, maybe Abigail H. O'Hagan would have had a different reception. As it was, my loyal aide was out on some errand, and the intruder slipped through the net.

The way she arrived ought to have warned me. There was this double-tap at the door, and I was still halfway through saying 'Come in' when she came in. No standing on ceremony for Abigail.

Not that I minded, at first. The young woman who breezed in, and stood there, hands on hips, was quite an eyeful.

Five feet five, with a tawny mane of gleaming hair that swung around almost at shoulder length when she moved her head. Hazel eyes glittered penetratingly either side of a firm, straight nose. Except for a trace of lipstick on the enquiring mouth, the lightly tanned face was devoid of make-up. The long-sleeved white blouse was tailored, to disappear inside a bottle green pleated skirt, which moulded itself carefully to the pleasing outline. My visitor weighed in at around one hundred and fifteen pounds, give or take an ounce, and every one of those pounds was placed where Nature ideally intended. She was around twenty-five or -six.

'I don't think you should,' she announced, 'so soon after lunch.'

Her voice was warm and resonant, and I hoped the entire conversation would not be conducted in riddles.

'Huh?' I managed, sounding rather foolish.

She had a devilish smile.

'I don't think you should eat me,' she explained. 'Not yet, anyway. That's what you had in mind, wasn't it?'

But I was recovering now. I was supposed to have the whip hand here. Dammit, it was my office. Having half risen from the chair, I now sat back and inspected her thoroughly. The second inspection was even more rewarding than the first.

'I have this rule about eating people I don't know,' I told her calmly. 'Maybe if we were introduced?'

'Sure.'

She swung a heavy green crocodile bag to the floor, pulled up a chair and sat down. The legs were finely shaped and straight, but she wasn't advertising them today.

'O'Hagan,' she announced brightly. 'I'm

3

Abigail H. O'Hagan. The First. And you're Preston. We meet at last.'

I nodded.

'So we do. What does the H. stand for?'

'I never tell. I only use it because so many men seem to think it's important to have a middle initial.'

That seemed to be some kind of explanation, in her book.

'I see. And the First? Why the First?'

'Why not?' she demanded pugnaciously. 'Plenty of men go around calling themselves the Third, or the Fourth. All that tells me is that they're not even originals. Just copies of earlier, better men. Well, I'm not one of those. I stand on my own two feet.'

When they recruited all the shrinking violets, my new friend had clearly been overlooked.

'Well O.K. Miss, or is it Mrs.—'

'You want to marry me?'

'Not at this moment. It's too soon after lunch,' I reminded her.

'Then mind your own business. Miz will do. Better still, call me Abigail.'

The mention of business seemed to give me a lead.

'Very well. Abigail it is. Now what can I do for you, Abigail?'

Instead of answering my question, she stared at me intently.

'Been looking forward to this,' she

4

announced. 'Got a list I keep at home. People I want to meet, when the time is right. You're on it.'

Trying not to look too pleased, I said. 'Really? Well, that's very flattering. Could I ask why?'

Her hand slapped suddenly against the desk top. It made me jump, but didn't prevent me from noticing the long, well-kept fingers.

'Like the way you handle yourself,' she confided. 'Always read what the papers have to say. Those crazy women a few months back, what was their name, Towers?—yes, Towers. That was creepy, huh? [*A Long Time Dead*] Some day, you must tell me what really happened out at that house.'

With such a direct female as this, I might easily find myself saying things I shouldn't, before I realised it.

'Maybe some day,' I said pleasantly. 'This is all very flattering Miz—er—Abigail, and I'm lapping it up, but you still haven't told me why you're here.'

'Right,' she agreed briskly. 'Oh, could I have one of those?'

Without thinking, I had tapped out a cigaret, and was about to push the pack away.

'Oh, sure.'

She took one, lit it from the flame I extended over the desk, then removed it from the inviting lips and read the legend.

'Old Favorites, huh? You smoke nothing but

5

the best.'

'And I have a list of charges to prove it,' I informed her. 'Now then, you were about to explain.'

'Yup. Well, there's this thing that's come up, you see, and since it involves your fair city, I thought, right. This is my chance. Deal with the problem, and meet Mark Preston, all at one go. Couldn't miss a chance like that, right?'

'Fine. So you're here. Do I gather from what you say, you don't live around here?'

'Lord, no. This is vacation country to me. Very pleasant, and all that, but not like a real working town. I'm from San Francisco.'

There was a time, years ago, when I would have risen to that particular bait. But that time was past, and I could no longer summon the energy to dispute the merits of our respective cities.

'A very fine city,' I acknowledged gravely.

Abigail eyed me suspiciously.

'No cracks about the smog?' she queried.

I shrugged.

'We're working quietly on our brand,' I explained. 'It's coming along very well. Now then, about this visit?'

'A bond jumper. We have to track him down.'

'Ah.'

I had picked up a pen in readiness for the details, but that 'we' gave me pause.

6

'People who jump their bonds are part of my routine business,' I admitted. 'When you say "we" have to find him, I imagine you don't mean that literally?'

She inclined her head. The shining mane divided into two arcs, swinging forward on either side of her face. She probably did it for effect, and it worked.

'You're wrong, Preston. I mean it quite literally. We do this together. You,' she pointed, 'and me. The bond is in the sum of twenty-five thousand dollars, so with the fee at the usual ten per cent, we get to split two thousand five hundred. Not bad, eh?'

The arithmetic was O.K. The reasoning was bad.

'Look, no offense, but why should I split with you? The details of this case will drift through the usual channels. Tomorrow, next day, I'll get a flier from the insurance people. I can go ahead without you.'

The gleaming hair went flying in all directions, as she wagged her head in vigorous denial.

'No chance,' she denied. 'This one is not going to be reported. So, it's me or nothing, you see?'

No, I did not see. Furthermore, I did not like the confident way she kept getting the better of me all the time. If I'd had a little more foresight, I ought to have realised I hadn't seen the half of it yet.

'Maybe you'd care to enlarge on that?' I invited.

'Oh sure. The guy involved is one Joseph P. McEvoy. You see what I mean? Even the bond jumpers claim the middle initial.'

I ignored that.

'What was McEvoy's job?'

'Payroll supervisor. The company still has a large weekly payroll in cash. Old Joseph collected from the bank as usual this week, and forgot to bring the money back to the company.'

'How much is missing?'

'Thirty-eight thousand plus.'

The story was so routine, it was almost boring. But it would take a better man than me to feel bored around this explosive female opposite. And there were several questions to be asked.

'Why doesn't the company report all this to the insurers?'

Her eyes gleamed wickedly.

'Several reasons. For one thing, good old Joseph has been a trusted employee for lo these many years. They don't really want him in jail, which is where the insurers would certainly put him.'

And where he certainly belongs, I finished mentally.

'All right, so they don't want good old trusty Joseph in jail, just because of this minor slip. How do you get involved?'

'I got the trace job,' she said triumphantly. 'I'm an attorney, did I mention that?'

My face must have registered something. Disbelief, dismay, something. She chuckled.

'I see that I hold your interest. Here, if you don't believe me.'

Diving into the green leather, she poked around and come up with a small card which she now presented triumphantly. I stared at it, and the legend assured me that she was what she claimed.

'Anyone can get cards printed,' I hedged.

Abigail snorted in the most unladylike fashion.

'Don't be such an old grouch. It's easy enough to check me out.'

I knew it would be no more than a formality.

'All right, so you're an attorney. It's an odd way to practise law, to travel several hundred miles, when all you needed to do was pick up a telephone. The rest of your cases will suffer, won't they?'

She pouted. I liked it.

'The rest of my cases? Huh?' There was that snort again. 'Let me tell you something, Preston. My home town is a fine place, but if you want to be a lawyer, you have to be a hundred years old, and a man. I'm going to have to ask you to take my word for it about my age, and—'

'You got it,' I confirmed. 'I had you pegged

9

for the early seventies, no more. As to the rest of it, a man you are not. I happen to be one of those myself, and I can always tell.'

Her eyes mocked me again.

'I'll bet. You want to discuss that any further?'

The subject was one that interested me very much, but I wished she would stick to the point for two consecutive sentences.

I shook my head, hopefully with conviction.

'Not right now. I'm up to here in unemployed seventy-year-old lady lawyers. How come you got this job?'

'The company took pity on me. They said, here's a nice piece of legal work for that firebrand lawyer, Abigail H. It'll get her started on that long road to the Supreme Court.'

'Very considerate of them. What company are we talking about?'

'The O'Hagan Machine Company,' she replied, deadpan.

I might have known.

'You did say O'Hagan?'

'Yes. My white-haired old daddy is the president. Just a coincidence.'

'Just so,' I went along. 'So this McEvoy worked for your father, and he took off with all this money. What makes you think he's here in Monkton?'

She shrugged expressively.

'A hunch. Strictly a female-type hunch. You see, a couple of years ago, there was a girl who

10

worked in McEvoy's section. She was about my age, a good deal younger than him—'

'—and how old would he be?' I interrupted.

'About your age,' she said impishly.

I winced, and invited her to continue.

'Well, McEvoy seemed to spend too much company time talking with this girl. You know how people notice things like that. McEvoy is married, and it wasn't going down too well with other staff. About six months ago, the girl quit the job, and it all seemed to fizzle out.'

'What reason did she give for leaving?'

'She said she was getting married. Nobody knew whether that was true or not. Nobody cared really, because the important thing was that the McEvoy situation was resolved. Anyway, she left. Then, when I heard about the money, I thought of her straight away. Joe McEvoy has twelve years' company service, and never put a foot wrong, except that he used to take too much interest in this girl. It struck me that if I could find her, I might find him, too. And the money, of course.'

'Of course.' I tapped idly with my fingers. 'It's probably unnecessary to ask, but have you thought about the more obvious angles?'

She cocked her head to one side, looking puzzled.

'Such as?'

'Well, his home life for one thing. You said he was married. Is there any money trouble at home? Is his wife a sick woman, for instance?

11

Those medical bills can really sink a man. Is he a gambler? That's another fast road to the poorhouse. That kind of thing.'

The headshake was slow but definite.

'No. Nothing of that kind. The bank gives him an A.O.K. He pays his bills, keeps one step ahead of the game, like most of the world.' Then her tone altered, became slightly aggressive. 'This is pretty elementary stuff, Preston. Did you think I wouldn't have checked out that kind of thing, before I came charging down here?'

Since that was exactly what I had been thinking, my denial must have sounded feeble.

'No, no. Just making sure, that's all.'

'Huh.' Abigail was unconvinced. 'Well, after' with heavy emphasis on the 'after'— 'after I checked the obvious possibilities, I remembered the girl. It would do no harm to find out what became of her after she quit the company. Say, isn't that the very devil?'

'What is?'

'Trying to trace someone's movements. I mean, you'd think it would be so simple. All people have to do is to give you the most elementary information. But will they? They stall, they fidget-ass around. You'd think they were being asked to betray their country, or something. Are they always like that?'

I grinned. It doesn't do any harm for the occasional outsider to find out how difficult it can be, acquiring a few simple facts.

'Not always,' I qualified, 'only most of the time. Anyway, you must have got some answers in the end, because you're here.'

That steered her back on course.

'Right. Well, after all my dogged perseverance, for which I claim maximum credit, I found she'd moved down here. I even have an address.'

She had the girl's name, and her address. I guess when a man has been in my line of work a few years, it sours his outlook. The obvious question was, why me?

'Abigail, you puzzle me,' I confessed. 'If you know who she is, and where she is, why should you want to give me twelve hundred and fifty dollars? You can probably get a cab for five bucks.'

If I'd been hoping to unsettle her, I was to be disappointed. She nodded enthusiastic agreement.

'Right on the button. Exactly what I figured when I flew down. I was going to call on you anyway, but that would have been to meet you, not to split the money.'

That made more sense.

'But something changed your mind,' I prompted. 'What?'

'The address,' she replied simply. 'I don't want to sound sour on your lovely city here, but that Conquest Street is something else. It's no place for a sweet old-fashioned gal even to set foot, leave alone asking questions.'

She was right about that, though I'd take a rain-check on her description of herself.

'Conquest is not featured in our tourist brochure,' I admitted. 'I imagine this place is in the high numbers?'

The hazel eyes narrowed.

'Now, how would you know that?'

'Because it's my town. This particular boulevard starts out in the business section, and it isn't too bad for the first block or so. After that, it's downhill and fast, which I presume is where you've been?'

'Right again. The number is seven o nine. It's a phoney anyway, so far as the girl is concerned. Not a living place at all. Full of one-room offices.'

'Ah. So we have a problem right away. What's this girl's name?'

'Sally Dewes.'

'I don't suppose you have a picture of her?'

'No. But I'll know her, don't worry.'

It would have been unkind to point out that we had to find her, before Abigail's recognition would be of much help.

'You said she left to get married. Is this her married name, Dewes?'

'No. It's her own. Maybe the marriage didn't come off. You know what these showbiz people are like.' Then seeing my expression, she explained, 'Oh, didn't I tell you about that? This man, the one she claimed was going to marry her, he had something to do with

14

entertainment. So she said.'

'But you didn't know his name?' I pressed.

'No. Well, what do you think?'

Abigail looked at me brightly, as if expecting some startling pronouncement. What did I think? I was wondering the same thing. An employee went missing from a position of trust with a bagful of somebody else's cash. According to Miss Fixit opposite, the chances were he would be found in Monkton City, four hundred miles away from home. And the only pointer she had was that Sally Dewes had moved down this way in the last six months, and to a phoney address at that. Any correspondence-course detective would show Abigail H. O'Hagan the door, and get back to his History of Fingerprints. But I don't happen to be one of those, and I've learned a few strange lessons over the years. One of them is about the unscientific area known as woman's intuition. I've seen them come up winners against the most irrefutable logic. Another area is a woman's understanding about other women. It's uncanny, the way they can get to the bottom of motives or actions. On top of all that, I liked this O'Hagan. I wanted her to win.

'Your nose says we'll learn something about Joseph P. McEvoy if we poke around Conquest Street, right?'

She wrinkled the described organ like a hunting dog.

15

'That's what it says,' she confirmed. 'You want to follow it?'

I stood up, and sighed.

'It's a pretty nose. I have a horrible feeling I'll probably follow it, wherever you go.'

She had a wicked grin.

'I'll bet you say that to all the schnozzles. Your car, right?'

'Right.'


# TWO

Some people say that even the name Conquest Street is a corruption. The original invaders of this part of the world were the Spanish, and many of the place names bear witness to their long settlement. Conquest is claimed to be a twisted version of Conquistadores, and I like to think there's some truth in that. It would be very fitting for the hub of all the city's vice and corruption to have acquired even its name by the same route.

Like every good whore, it looks inviting from a distance. It starts off on a high note, with a legit theatre right on the corner with Fourth Street. Inside there are real live actors, people who have to learn the words by heart before they go on. That is the only contact with reality. After that the street level falls away, and the premises fall right along with it.

It's downhill all the way to Crane Street. It's the pin-ball parade, dives alternating with joints alternating with rat-traps. Music live, music canned, smells of every type of ethnic cooking, girls, lights, bars. And always more girls. They say that there's no kind of mistake you can't make on Conquest Street, and people keep pouring in to check out the resources. It's no place for the unwary, once the sun goes down.

Even in the daylight, it's no place for a woman, except that kind of woman. Whatever kind of kook she might be Abigail was definitely not in the Conquest category. The only thing that surprised me was that she had enough sense to recognise the fact, and not go charging in alone. I was still at the stage, you see, where Abigail could surprise me.

The sun was starting its nosedive towards the sea when I pulled up outside number seven o nine. The neon forest had already been switched on, but against the natural sunlight it only looked tawdry and despairing. One or two of the joints were already in business, hoping to catch the early suckers. The suckers were around too, anxious to be caught. It had been in my mind to leave Abigail in the car while I took a preliminary sniff around, but the little mind-reader was out and waiting before I could speak.

Seven o nine was no more than an open doorway, dividing a greasy spoon and a topless

17

disco. In the narrow hallway the various enterprises pursued by the proud tenants were displayed on postcards stuck to the wall with thumbtacks. Most of them were handwritten, but one was printed, and it read 'Nite-Spot Features—Second Floor. A. Schwarz. Prop.' Abigail had said the girl had been talking about a man in show business, and we had to start somewhere. I pointed to the card with my finger, and looked at her enquiringly.

'Could be,' she agreed.

'One thing,' I told her, 'let me do the talking. O.K.?'

'You got it, coach.'

There had been a lot of traffic up those battered wooden stairs, and our feet clumped noisily as we went up. On the first landing, a door led off to the right, which would put the office above the topless disco. There was enough of the black lettering left on the door to identify it as the one we wanted. I knocked and opened it.

A man looked up from a farmhouse table which doubled as a desk. His face was shrewd and swarthy, with piercing black eyes, and he'd had the whole thing about forty years.

'Mr. Schwarz?'

'That's me. Antonio Schwarz, Proprietor, like it says downstairs.'

'Antonio?'

It was out before I realised it. He nodded quickly.

'That's it. You got any jokes I haven't heard before, I'll be surprised. And I'm not responsible for my parents.'

He was talking to me, but he was looking at Abigail, like any normal man would. Mr. Schwarz wasn't looking at his first woman, to judge by the rows of glossy photographs decorating the wall behind his head. They were all publicity pictures of dames in provocative poses, and in various stages of undress, including total. It was fairly obvious what kind of features were being presented by the night spots served by Nite-Spot Features.

'We're looking for a girl—'

'Just a minute,' he chipped in, 'this ain't fair. You got my name, right? Do you have one of your own?'

'Preston. I'm Mark Preston. This girl is having her mail sent here. She obviously doesn't live here, so I want to know where to find her. Her name is Dewes, Sally Dewes.'

He screwed up his forehead in massive concentration.

'Dewes? No, I don't believe I ever heard the name. Somebody give you a wrong number, buddy. What did she do, this Dewes?'

'Do? I didn't say she did anything,' I objected.

'Aw nuts,' he scoffed, 'you're some kind of copper, right? Who else would come here with this kind of stuff?'

It was evident from his tone that Antonio

19

Schwarz was about to close the file on me. There was a little squeal of laughter, which made us both look at Abigail.

'He's always like this,' she announced, in a grating voice pitched half an octave higher than her normal warm tone. 'Ain't it terrible? It's enough to get a girl a bad name, having her big brother go around making noises like a pig.'

Schwarz turned his face gladly towards her, drinking her in openly.

'This is your brother?'

'Oh, sure. I didn't want him to come down here, but he said he didn't want me down this street by myself. I told him, I said, brother dear, if you'd seen some of the joints I worked in, I said, you'd like to have a fit.'

'Oh?'

Schwarz looked at me for a reaction. Annoyance was struggling inside me with amusement at this strident hoyden who'd promised to let me do all the talking. As a result, my face probably looked perplexed. It seemed to satisfy Schwarz.

'What's your name, girlie?'

Well, she asked for it. 'Girlie' was just right for this new Abigail. She pouted and shrugged.

'You mean my given name, or my perfessional name?'

That was what she said, perfessional.

'Well your per—your stage name, naturally. I didn't know you were in the business.'

'I should just hope,' she squealed. 'All my life, that's all. I'm Sugar Plum Preston. Listen, I go way back to the original Tallulah's Tiny Tots. You remember them?'

'Why, sure,' lied Schwarz heartily, 'a great act. Great.'

Abigail minced across the room and perched sideways on his desk. The great impresario was given a much greater display of legs than a certain private investigator had received. He didn't miss them, either.

'I got a little big for it, Tony,' she advised him confidentially. 'They couldn't keep me inside those costumes any more. Know what I mean?'

She angled herself against the light, so that nobody could be in any doubt. The little guy loved it.

'So you moved on, huh?' he prompted.

'Yup. I was one of the original Marx Sisters, did you know? Psycho, Wino and Nympho. We played every joint on the Eastern Seaboard. You can guess which one was me, if you want.'

Abigail flexed her back muscles, turning sideways on to the little agent. His eyes almost popped out of his head.

'Yeah,' he breathed. 'I can believe. So what's all this with the Sally Dewes bit?'

'We're old friends,' claimed Sugar Plum. 'I been doing a single, but it's kind of lonely. Thought maybe Sally and me could put something together.'

Antonio looked over at me.

'Look,' he said, confidentially, 'Sugar Plum ain't gonna come to no harm with me. I mean, I'm a business man, right?'

'So?'

'So I'd like a chance to talk with her alone. Just business chat, you know how it is. Kind of confidential. Would you mind?'

I squared my brotherly shoulders, looking doubtful. I wasn't worried about anything happening to Abigail. What was concerning me was little Schwarz's welfare, if he got out of line.

'Well—' I hesitated.

'Aw go on, you old grouch. I'll be out in just a couple minutes.'

Sugar Plum Abigail put her head on one side, and appealed to me. It was a trick I was already beginning to recognise. Trouble was, I liked it.

'Well O.K.,' I agreed grudgingly. 'Five minutes, and that's tops.'

I went out. As I pulled the door behind me, I heard her say—

'He's just a sweet old grouch, really. Now then, Tony—'

My feet echoed on the stairs again. The light outside was now fading fast. I went and sat in the car, watching the open doorway, and the window above the topless disco, which had to be the Schwarz office. Abigail's performance up there had me rethinking our

22

relationship. She certainly behaved like a girl who could look after herself, even on Conquest Street. But I mustn't lose sight of the fact that I had been around while she did it. It could have been my presence that gave her the extra confidence. It gave me something to chew over during a long five minutes.

I was on the point of going back to get her, when she appeared suddenly in the doorway. Walking quickly across she climbed in and slumped against the seat.

'Did you notice that little Schwarz was deformed?' she demanded.

'No, I didn't spot it,' I admitted.

'Well, he is. That man has six hands. Three on each arm.'

I grinned without sympathy.

'The way you were pushing the product, you can't complain if the customers want to buy.'

She glared at me.

'Sour grapes,' she scoffed. 'You weren't going to get anywhere with that approach of yours. Somebody had to do something constructive.'

'So what did you get? Outside of the pawmarks, I mean.'

'The little man doesn't know Sally. Any mail that comes for her gets picked up by her man-friend. Name of Jack Durrant, does it mean anything?'

I shook my head.

'Not right off the top,' I confessed. 'Any

more about him?'

'He's one of those personality kid types. Little of everything, you know? He can sing a song, tell a few gags, host up a cabaret. That kind of stuff. There's a dozen like him on every street corner. Now and then, one of them is in the right place at the right time. Next thing you know, they just take off. Their own chat show, the whole bit. That's Jack Durrant.'

'Sounds harmless enough. And he's, what shall we say, Sally Dewes' protector?'

'For want of a better word. The point is, if we want the girl, first we have to find him. Schwarz didn't have an address, but he knows where the guy is working.'

'All we need. Where is it?'

'Place called the Bear Bear Club. You know it?'

I thought for a moment, then shook my head.

'Nothing happens. These places open and fold like a morning paper. It probably opened last week. Next week it'll just be a memory. You didn't happen to get the address?'

Abigail gave me one of her snorts.

'Listen, I had to go through a major assault to get this much. This is your town, you get the address, right?'

'I'll think of something.'

I drove out of the district to a bar where a girl can sit unmolested, at least for the duration of one phone call. Abigail surprised me by asking for a glass of California white wine. I'd have to put her down as a Barleycorn Special at least, on her recent showing. Only we weren't Sugar Plum any longer. We were now Hawkshaw O'Hagan, hot on the villain's heels.

'We ought to talk about how we're going to handle this Durrant,' she said importantly.

'Handle him? How do you mean, handle him?'

She looked at me with pity.

'We have to be careful,' she explained. 'Don't want to frighten the guy off. Don't forget, he's all we have. Once we lose him, we're back out there in the jungle, with no machete.'

I wondered where this girl dug up those metaphors.

'We know nothing against the guy,' I protested. 'All he does is to pick up the mail for his girl-friend. All the girl-friend ever did was to look pretty enough for some other guy to make sheeps' eyes at, months and months ago. That doesn't exactly qualify them both for Murder Incorporated.'

'So you say,' she sneered. 'You forget, the man with the sheeps' eyes blew town with thirty-eight big ones.'

I shook my head feebly, in the face of what she undoubtedly saw as unassailable logic.

'But we don't know there's any connection.

We're just stumbling around, keeping our fingers crossed.'

Abigial made it obvious that she was exercising great patience with me.

'So you say,' she repeated. 'Anyway, you didn't answer my question. What do you propose to do when you stumble across this Jack Durrant?'

I pretended to consider this very carefully. Then I said—

'Well, how's this? I'll go up to him, and I'll say "Good evening, Mr. Durrant. I'm rather anxious to contact Sally Dewes, and perhaps you might tell me where I'll find her".'

'Just like that?' sneered Hawkshaw.

'What would you suggest? A rubber hose?'

'I never heard anything so elementary,' she scoffed. 'How'd you ever get this big reputation? You must bribe all the newspaper reporters.'

I retreated into my scotch for a breather.

'The only way to get answers to questions, is to ask them in the first place,' I explained carefully. 'That's how this game operates. A question here, an answer there, gradually you build up some kind of picture. Most of it is very routine, boring almost. You can't go around on the assumption that every other citizen is the Boston Strangler.'

'So you'll just ask him right out?'

'Yes.'

'The way you did with little Schwarzie?

Look how far that got you.'

She looked positively cock-a-hoop now.

'The Schwarz thing would have come out all right, if you'd kept quiet the way you promised. We didn't need all that fan dance routine.'

Abigail smiled maddeningly.

'All I know is, you got nothing. I got the information required. Which, by the way, you still haven't converted to an address.'

I looked around at the quiet, well-behaved, early evening drinkers.

'I'm going to make a phone call,' I told her. 'Do you think you can manage not to set fire to the place while I'm gone?'

She fluttered her eyebrows and twittered.

'Why, Mr. Preston, Ah don't have the slightest idea what you're going on about. Ah'm just gonna sit here, supping at this ole julep.'

Giving her one last threatening look, I went out to the row of payphones at the back. When I returned, I was relieved to find her alone, sipping decorously at her wine.

'My, that was quick. Did you get it?'

I nodded, finishing up my drink.

'It's a place that used to be called the Old Log Cabin, out in Lake Valley. I've been there a couple of times in the past.'

She wanted to know how I got the information, without at the same time letting me see she was impressed. Truth was, there's nothing to it. All you have to do is know people. It was a cinch the place would have a telephone. I know one or two people in the telephone company, and all I need to do in a case like that is ask them. The old direct question routine. The same one I intended to use on Jack Durrant, nothing mysterious about it.

Trying to sound casual, she said—

'How did you manage to get hold of the address so quickly?'

I tapped significantly at the side of my nose.

'You have to have sources, in this business.'

Her eyes glinted at this frustration, but she wasn't going to plead. The hell with her, I thought, it'll do her no harm.

'Well, if we're going for a ride, we'd better get on with it,' she said, changing the subject.

I looked at my watch. It was only eight fifteen.

'There's no point in going out there just yet,' I demurred. 'I know what these places are like. If there's some kind of show going on, it won't be earlier than ten o'clock. We can't just spend all that time drinking out there.'

'So what's the alternative?' she countered. 'Do we spend all that time drinking here, instead?'

'No, we don't. I thought it would be a good idea if I dropped you off at your hotel. It'll give you an opportunity to unpack your bag. I'll go back to my place, see if I can track down

28

another shirt. Pick you up around nine thirty, nine forty-five. What do you say?'

On the point of saying something, she changed her mind and nodded.

'O.K. Let's go.'

We got back to the car, and I switched on.

'Which way, lady?'

'I don't know,' she admitted.

'Well, what's the name of the place?'

She fidgeted with her hands, and muttered something.

'What's that? I didn't catch what you said.'

Turning towards me, she switched on one of her Sunnybrook Farm smiles.

'It's called Parkside Towers.'

Must be new, I decided.

'Don't know any hotel by that name,' I admitted. 'Oddly enough, that's the name of my apartment block.'

'Yes, it is,' she agreed.

I don't know why it should have taken me a full three seconds to register the implication of that. She couldn't be serious. Then I looked at that angelic smile. She could be serious.

'You can't be serious,' I said, without conviction.

'Why not? You have this great big luxurious apartment, all to yourself. I'm just a poor struggling lawyer, with no money and no place to go. What are partners for, tell me that?'

'Don't give me all that Orphan Annie,' I snapped. 'Your daddy owns half of San

Francisco, you told me so yourself.'

'That has nothing to do with it,' she pouted. 'My daddy has a rule, for all his kids. If they want to be rich, they have two alternatives. Either they can get out in the world and get their own, or they can wait until he dies, and see what Santa Claus brings. Until then, nothing. He brought us up to be people, not rich kids.'

O'Hagan père sounded like an interesting character.

'Did he tell you it's O.K. to go around bumming off every character you pick up in bars?' I queried nastily.

She looked demure, at that. It was infuriating.

'Why Mr. Preston, how you do go on. You know perfectly well, I made a formal call at your business premises.'

'That doesn't make it all right for you to make an informal stay at my domestic premises,' I refuted. 'Besides, I don't have enough room.'

'Huh,' she dismissed. 'Don't be such an old meanie. Besides, you're taking too much for granted. I'm going to sleep on the couch.'

'Damn right you are,' I agreed. 'You needn't think—what am I saying? I haven't agreed to this. Besides, there's your suitcase. Where is it?'

'In the back of the car,' she smiled sweetly. 'This is really awfully good—'

30

'What do you mean, in the back?' I grouched. 'How did you know which car was mine?'

'Oh, I didn't. The lot attendant, he knew. He's a very nice man, you know? Did he tell you he has this sick sister—'

'No,' I snarled, 'and don't think you're going to get away with this. There isn't time to get you fixed up before we call on this Durrant, so O.K. You can come in and fix your face, or whatever. But as soon as we're through at the Bear Bear Club, we're going and find you a place to flop. Understood?'

'Well, I think you're a proper old meanie. But it shall be even as you say, o vizier.'

'Damn right,' I grumbled.

## THREE

At the apartment, she behaved herself very well, and I began to feel more easy in my mind. She had to poke around the place, but that's only natural in any woman, and I knew she'd be checking the linen-drawers when she thought I wasn't looking.

'But it's beautiful,' she admired. 'Must cost you a small fortune.'

'It comes from asking questions,' I replied. 'You ask enough, and get a high percentage of the right answers, and presto—here you are.'

31

She wasn't going to rise to that one, but prowled off into the small kitchen.

'Hey, there's no food in here,' she called.

I went in after her, and opened a cupboard. There were all my supplies, neatly lined up. Extra coffee, two reserve bottles of scotch, and a large carton of Old Favorites.

'Everything a man needs,' I defended.

'H'm.'

She rested a hand lightly on my lapel, smiling ruminatively. I wondered what was running through her mind, but I wasn't going to run the risk of asking. Instead, I switched subjects.

'We live a spartan life here,' I told her. 'Just the one bathroom. You want to go first?'

'I could do with some freshening,' she admitted. 'Will you be making any coffee?'

That would put her in the bathroom, and me in the kitchen. A good arrangement.

'Yes,' I confirmed, perhaps a little too heartily. 'Yes, I've been meaning to clean up in here, as well. Now's as good a time as any.'

Ten minutes later, I heard her making coming-out-of-the bathroom noises. I kept my back squarely towards the open kitchen door, while she located her bag, and disappeared with it into the bedroom. The coffee was ready, and it seemed to me my hand could have been a little steadier as I poured myself the first cup. My turn for the bathroom, and I tossed my jacket onto a chair as I went in.

32

There were alien smells in there. Alien, but nice. The kind of nice you only get when there's a woman around. I was glad to get out there, and parked in a solid male chair. First, I poured out more coffee, having found and dusted off my most presentable beaker.

'Coffee up,' I called.

'Coming.'

It was ridiculous that I should feel nervous this way. I was in charge here. This was my apartment, and that was my coffee steaming in my beakers. She was the intruder, this Abigail, smelling up the place and generally creating an aura of—of what?

'Smells good.'

It was evidently cherry-picking time. She wore a full-sleeved cherry-colored top in some shining material, cherry ski pants and white sneakers. Her face radiated freshness and good health. So did the rest of her. Walking over to me, she picked up her coffee, and sipped.

'Magic,' she sighed, and sat down.

I'd been going to offer a cigaret anyway, but she didn't wait for that. She simply leaned over, cool as you please, took one, and waited for me to light it. Anybody would think she lived there.

Now, she leaned back comfortably in the padded chair, sighed, and inspected me carefully through a haze of drifting smoke.

'You've done very well,' she decided.

33

What did she mean? My standard of living? My coffee-making?

'Huh?' I queried.

'Plenty of men would have made a heavy play for me long before this,' she explained. 'I've been at about maximum vulnerability these past thirty minutes, what with the bathroom and then the bedroom. Why didn't you?'

I'd been wondering the same thing. Well, I might as well score maximum credits, while the chance presented.

'I'm not an opportunist in that area,' I explained solemnly. 'I don't just grab at anything that passes by.'

She nodded thoughtfully.

'Maybe,' she half-agreed. 'I was wondering if there was anything wrong with me? Some people think I'm not half-bad.'

'I agree with some people,' I conceded, 'but you and I are here on business, remember? So, let's drink up and be on our way.'

Evidently reluctant to leave the subject, she shrugged, and applied herself to the coffee.

'Tell me about Lake Valley. It's quite a beauty spot, isn't it?'

'I'll tell you in the car. It gets cold out there at night. You'll need some kind of coat.'

She had some kind of coat, a padded affair in faded red denim. It was a garment you only saw on long-haul truck drivers, or young women who wished they looked like Abigail H.

O'Hagan. Settling herself comfortably beside me in the car, she said—

'You were going to tell me about Lake Valley.'

I told her the old tale about Captain Ramon Hernandez and his troop of soldiers. They'd come roaring and rampaging up from the south, in fifteen hundred and something. By the time they arrived at our piece of the coast, they'd already been away from the old country more than three years. They were no longer the crack troops who'd set out on the voyage originally. Now, they were a half-disciplined gang of ruffians, well skilled in the loot, rape and murder business. They had so much gold that it took a train of two hundred Indians to carry it all, and the crossing of the lake presented a big problem. Hernandez decided to build a flotilla of rafts, and the next two months were spent in the building of this fleet. The Indians didn't like the idea. They were already hundreds of miles from home, and now they would be leaving forever, the way they saw it. They knew the world ended in a big water, and decided the lake was the one. Until that time, they had been in no position to argue with the superior weapons carried by the invaders. Bows and arrows and wooden spears had proved to be no match for the heavy metal swords and crossbows, to say nothing of the firing pieces. But on the big water, things would be different. There would be twenty of the floating logplatforms, each carrying twelve to fifteen men, and supporting equipment. When they finally set off, it was the signal for the only recorded naval battle fought by the North American Indians. The whole fleet wound up at the bottom of the lake. Most of the Indians made it to the shore, but there is no record that any of the Spaniards escaped. The loot wound up on the lake-bed, and it is now an integral part of life in those parts, that the latest treasure expedition sets up camp.

Abigail listened to all this without interrupting. Then she said—

'Did you know you can't travel a hundred miles in any direction along this coastline without hearing some kind of version of that tale?'

I grinned in the darkness.

'Don't hold me responsible just because a lot of other people get jealous of our local folklore. What you've been hearing here is the genuine article.'

An illuminated bill board loomed up at the roadside.

'Well,' she said grudgingly, 'at least it got us out here. According to that sign, the Bear-Bear Club is two miles ahead. First time I've seen it written down. I was a little worried about how they'd spell "bear".'

A couple of minutes later, I turned into the large forecourt of the club. The previous

36

owners had spent some money creating a frontier look to the place. There was no need for that to be altered under the new title, so the current owners had simply stuck an effigy of an eight-foot grizzly on the roof. It was almost ten o'clock, and the place was going to be busy, judging by the number of cars outside.

We went up the wooden steps, and into the main entrance. Except for the odd tomahawk stuck to the walls, and the bear motif here and there, the place was like a hundred other eat-and-shuffle establishments.

'Good evening, sir. Do you have a reservation?'

I was getting used to people addressing me with their mouths, and Abigail with their eyes.

'No, this was a last-minute decision,' I told the captain. Then I held out a nice, crisp tenspot. 'Would there by any problem with a table?'

His fingers closed over the note like a sprung steel trap.

'Oh no sir, I'm sure we can fit you in.'

He led us to a table one row back from the matchbox dance floor. I didn't want some rock and roll champion kicking over my drink. Then we got settled down, and the waiter handed over printed menus which were almost as big as the table. I had no intention of running up a bill.

'Would you like to order now?'

'No,' I hedged. 'Maybe later. Right now, I'll

settle for a drink.'

I looked a warning at my dinner companion, who winked at the waiter.

'He has this stomach condition,' she confided. 'However, there's nothing wrong with me or my appetite. Now, I'm sure all this food is lovely, but why don't you just advise me what's looking best out in the kitchen tonight?'

She flashed the waiter one of her brilliant smiles, and he was her man from that moment. There was a little flag on his lapel with the name Paul on it.

This was getting out of hand. I'd seen the prices, and it was not my ambition to buy the place. In a last-ditch stand to save the situation, I said quickly—

'The Chef's Special is very highly spoken of.'

That at least is a fixed menu at a stated charge, no extras. Abigail sneered openly.

'Cheapskate,' she snapped. 'And on my birthday too.'

She looked up at Paul, who smiled lovingly, and darted a malevolent glance at me. Then he bowed, pointing at the card.

'The oysters are especially delicious, if I may suggest.'

'Oh, lovely. I'm wild about oysters. And then what do you think?'

I was out of it. They had their heads together now, and there was a lot of eye-rolling and lipsmacking, as they worked their way through the card. By the time they were finished, there was enough food on order to keep a beleaguered garrison for a week.

Paul raised his head, and inspected me with quiet triumph.

'Perhaps the gentleman's constitution would withstand a plain omelette?'

'No,' I said churlishly. 'It would withstand a very large scotch with plenty of ice.'

He drew himself up, collected another wink, and went away.

'No wonder your father threw you out,' I hissed. 'He probably couldn't afford to feed you.'

That brought me a wagging finger.

'Wouldn't have had you figured for a tightwad, Preston. It mars your image, that kind of thing.'

'We came here to work, not eat,' I reminded her.

As it turned out, the floorshow did not go on until eleven fifteen. That presented no problem to my charming companion, who spent the entire time packing away food like a starving python.

Finally the band struck up a chord, and the leader spoke into the microphone.

'And now folks, the Bear-Bear Club proudly presents cabaret time and who better to introduce it than your very favorite master of ceremonies, Jack Durrant.'

Roll on the drums, a light scatter of

39

applause, and out tripped the man we'd come to see. He was thirty years old, handsome in a flashy way, like a ball-player gone to seed. His speaking voice was pleasant, and he soon had the crowd in a good mood, with a barrage of quickfire political gags.

'He's good, isn't he?' whispered Abigail.

'He's no amateur,' I agreed.

The little show lasted for thirty minutes. Then, a final wave from a spotlit Durrant, and it was everybody dance.

'Wait here,' I instructed. 'I'll go and have a word with our man.'

For a moment I thought she'd give me an argument, but instead she nodded.

'I could use some more coffee, anyway.'

Working my way between the tables, I made for the curtained doorway through which the M.C. had exited. It led to a narrow corridor, which was strictly functional. I was wondering which of three doors to open when a blonde girl in street clothes came walking towards me. I recognised her as being the one who did the crazy juggling in the floorshow.

'Hi,' she greeted. 'Looking for the man's room?'

'No. I wanted to see Jack Durrant.' Then, remembering, I added hastily, 'Thought you were great out there tonight.'

Some of the tiredness went from her face.

'Oh really? Thank you. I sometimes wonder whether anyone is even looking. What do you

40

want Jack for? Not a tee vee job, is it? Listen, I have some special material.'

'No,' I denied quickly. 'This is just personal. Where will I find him?'

But she'd lost interest already.

'In there, if you're quick. Otherwise, the nearest bar.'

'Thanks.'

'There' was a door at the end. I went along, knocked, and stuck my head inside. My quarry was standing by a coat rack, with an upended bottle of whisky to his mouth. He turned at the interruption, and pulled the bottle away. Some of the firewater ran down his chin.

'Don't you ever knock?'

'I did,' I assured him. 'Like a word with you, Mr. Durrant.'

He didn't like that too well. Close to, his heavy features were even more puffy than they seemed on the stage.

'What kind of a word? Who are you?'

'Name is Preston, Mark Preston. I'm a private investigator, and—'

'If you're one of those, you'll have a license.'

I don't get upset any more, when people ask for my I.D. Sometimes, the sight of those official rubber stamps, and the libellous photograph, help to carry more weight. I pulled out my sticker and held it out for him to inspect. He peered at it, grunted and shrugged.

'So?'

'I'm trying to trace a young woman, and I

think you can help me. Her name is Dewes. Sally Dewes.'

His features screwed up, in that I'm-trying-to-recall fashion. Then he shook his head.

'No. Nothing comes through, feller. I don't know her. What kind of act does she have?'

I looked non-committal.

'Just this one specialty, that I know of. She gets people four hundred miles away to put things in envelopes, and send them to her. The truth is, she doesn't get them herself. She has a man do it for her. You're that man.'

Maybe I was being too obscure. If he looked puzzled before, he was positively bewildered now.

'I don't get it.'

'It's called the mail. The old Post Office gag. You must have heard of it. People write Sally letters, and you collect them from 709 Conquest Street.'

That got through. A kind of mottled purple stained the lower part of his face.

'Me? Hogwash. If Schwarz told you that, he's lying.'

'Come on, Durrant. Why would the little guy bother to tell me lies? It's no big deal in his life. I don't know why you're making such a mystery out of all this. Just let me talk to the girl. I won't keep her five minutes.'

A new voice spoke from behind me.

'Everything O.K. Mr. Durrant? This man bothering you?'

42

I turned, to look at a thickset man standing casually in the doorway. He was three inches shorter than me, but about eight inches wider, and all of it packed, solid muscle. The blonde juggler must have tipped him off. Durrant gave a short laugh.

'Hello Felix. No, there's no trouble. This customer was looking for a friend, but I can't help him. He was just leaving.'

Felix looked me up and down, easing weight on to the forward muscles of his feet. He was all set to show me back to my table, break my ribs, or merely toss me out through the skylight. The feeling that he could probably do it did nothing for my self-esteem.

I smiled at him pleasantly.

'Well, no harm done. I'll get back to my dinner.'

'You do that,' assented Durrant heavily.

When I got back into the club, most of the crowd were gathered thickly around the edge of the dance floor. The band was thrashing away in fine style, but I hadn't time to stop and see what was going on. I wanted to collect Abigail, and get out of there.

The table was empty. Well, not quite. Her evening purse lay in the center, and no woman would leave without her purse. She'd probably taken advantage of my absence to go and comb her hair or something. I was about to sit down and wait, when the crowd behind me began to clap hands in time with the music.

Might as well see what the big attraction was, I decided. Moving to the rear of the crowd, I edged around until I could see onto the floor.

The big attraction was Abigail. She and some tow-headed kid in jeans were really going to work on the music, and the crowd was loving it. The number came to an end, and the handclapping turned into enthusiastic applause. Abigail kissed her partner on the cheek, ruffled his hair, and muttered something to him. He laughed, and smacked her on the rump. Then she bowed quickly to the crowd, and began to make her way through. I just made it back to the table before she saw me.

'Oh hi,' she greeted. Her eyes were shining, and her face was flushed. She looked like a health ad. 'You were quick.'

'Not quick enough,' I grumbled. 'You're supposed to dance with the guy that brung you.'

That brought me a rich chuckle.

'C'm on, Mark. You don't really think you're any competition for that boy, do you? He was tri-state runner-up last year.'

'Really? Were you his partner then, too?'

I was sounding more old-maidish by the minute.

'Me? Lord, no. He's out of my class. I made it to the home state semi-final, though. I don't practise enough, that's my trouble.'

A group of people stopped beside us on the

44

way back to their table.

'Great show there, honey.'

'You really socked it to 'em.'

'Congratulations.'

She beamed all round, and said 'thank you' several times.

'That was fun,' she announced. 'Now then, how did you get on with our friend?'

'No progress,' I reported. 'He denies even knowing the girl. Then when I wanted to give him an argument, the club bouncer showed, and the discussion, as they say, came to an end.'

'You got the heave, h'm?' Her eyes mocked me. 'You don't seem to be very successful in the question department, do you? Want me to go and take a crack at it?'

'No. If you're finished trying to empty every cooking pot in the place, I want to leave.'

To my surprise, she didn't want to argue.

'Ready when you are, coach.'

I signalled to Paul, and he produced the check with a flourish. Emptying most of my wallet onto the silver tray, I motioned Abigail to lead the way out. A number of heads turned as she threaded her way between the tables, and one or two people even clapped. Outside in the foyer, she turned to me with a triumphant smile, and squeezed nay hand.

'That was fun, huh? We'll do it again, won't we?'

She was too much for me, totally irresistable. The size of the bill and the fair-headed boy both went out of my head. I only grinned back, and said—

'I shouldn't be at all surprised.'

In the car, she leaned her head against my shoulder. She smelled good.

'Tell me something. Why don't we just sit here, and wait for our friend Durrant to come out? It's a reasonable bet he's living with Sally Dewes. If so, he'll lead us straight to her.'

I started the motor.

'Two reasons why not,' I explained. 'First, he has another show to do, at one thirty. By the time that's finished, it'll be two a.m. at least. Even then, he may stay around here, drinking and chewing the fat. We could be sitting here three hours or more, and I have no ambition to do that.'

The tawny head moved up and down.

'Makes sense. That's one reason. You said there were two.'

We were out on the highway now, and the full moon was lighting up the scrubland on either side. It was very peaceful.

'The other reason is even more important, and something I'm going to have to look into. The bouncer called him Mr. Durrant.'

As an explanation, it was obviously insufficient.

'So? That's his name isn't it?'

'You don't understand. Durrant isn't some big-name entertainer, and that joint isn't in the big league. He's just an M.C., and in the

46

pecking order that puts him in about the same category as the captain of waiters and the band-leader. To the rest of the help he'll be Jack, or buddy, or hey-you. He will not be Mr. Durrant.'

'I don't get it,' she mumbled. 'You say he won't be, but he is. That makes you wrong, doesn't it?'

'No,' I assured her. 'It makes Mr. Durrant something more than an M.C. Like maybe the manager, or even one of the owners.'

Abigail sat up suddenly, and I missed her in the shoulder area.

'This could be good,' she said softly. 'Are you thinking what I'm thinking?'

'I don't know. Try me.'

She dived a hand in my pocket, feeling around for cigarets. Then she pulled out the pack, and lit one.

'I must buy some of my own,' she reflected, half to herself.

'Yes, you must,' I agreed. 'Now then, tell me this great theory.'

Leaning back against the leather, she fanned out smoke contentedly.

'Well, here's an M.C. called Mr. Durrant, for some reason. He has a girl, although he denies it. The girl used to be involved with another man. This other man just disappeared, with a great deal of money. The Bear-Bear Club has just re-opened, under new management. That costs money, doesn't it? If

47

the missing money somehow found its way down here, that could explain how an M.C. comes to be called mister, couldn't it? That's what I'm thinking, anyway.'

I turned towards her, and smiled.

'I'm thinking something similar,' I agreed. 'And there's a man I want to talk to about it.'

'Ah. Can I come, too?'

'I'm counting on it,' I assured her. 'This guy will love you.'


# FOUR

It was a little after twelve thirty in the a.m. when I pulled up outside the Oyster's Cloister. It was just about the end of the really busy time, and the man I had come to see could probably spare me a minute or two.

The Cloister is the top eating house for miles around, but it's no place to take a modest income. You had better know you are getting the best food in the state, and the prices are in the same top bracket. The place is owned and run by an old friend of mine, Reuben Krantz.

I hadn't darkened that particular door in an age, and Biff, the doorman, did a double take when he saw who it was.

'Hey Mr. Preston. Nice. This is nice. Where you been hiding?'

I punched him lightly in the ribs. It was a few years now since he'd been a middleweight contender, but he was still in good shape.

'Here and there,' I hedged, 'you know how it is. Like you to meet a friend of mine, Miss O'Hagan. Abigail, this is my friend—'

'Biff Halloran,' she finished, holding out her hand. 'This is a real pleasure. I'm a great fights fan, you know, and I remember you well from my high-school days. You haven't aged a day.'

The old pug was beside himself at the reception he had from my beautiful companion. He didn't know whether to take off his uniform cap, kiss her hand, or just go down on one knee.

'Pleased to meecha, Miss O'Hagan. A pleasure, believe me.'

'All mine,' she assured him. 'Wait till I tell my father I met Biff Halloran. He'll be green.'

It was too dark to see whether Biff was actually slobbering when I dragged her away from him and inside the foyer.

'Now listen,' I urged, 'this man we're going to see is named Reuben Krantz. Just don't foul it up for me. He's a very prominent man in certain quarters, and I don't have that many friends I can afford to lose any.'

She looked at me wide-eyed.

'Don't know what you mean,' she huffed. 'Soul of discretion, that's me. Listen, I won the dignity badge three straight years.'

'You must have bribed the judges,' I said

snidely. 'Now here's his office. Just leave it to me.'

There was a radio broadcast of a fight in progress when we entered the room. Ben Krantz sat half sideways to the door, and didn't bother to look up. Instead, he waved an arm around, with the presumable intention of our sitting down. We did that, and I was able to get my first look at him in months.

In his early fifties, Krantz had a shock of silver grey hair above a smooth tanned face. A tall man, with broad shoulders and a narrow waist, he still moved with an athletic grace more appropriate to a man twenty years younger.

He looked like what he was, a prosperous, well-connected business man. He also looked as if he'd been born to it, which he hadn't. Ben was very much from the other side of the tracks, and he's come over them with a wild reputation and iron fists. Some of his exploits back in those days would have made the hair stand up on the heads of the prosperous people eating outside in his celebrated restaurant. But it had all been a long time ago, and there were not many people around who knew him as anything but the solid citizen he was now.

Abigail was looking him over too, and seemed to be liking what she saw. I chuckled inwardly at what I knew and she didn't. There was an outburst of noise from the radio. Ben clucked with annoyance, switched off, and

50

banged his hand down on the gleaming table.

'Creampuffs,' he announced. 'They wouldn't have had enough moxy for a newspaper round in my day—oh.'

He'd seen me, and carried on talking. Now he saw Abigail, and stopped.

'Ben, this is Abigail O'Hagan, a lawyer friend from San Francisco.'

Ben was already on his feet and walking round the desk to greet her.

'How do you do, Miss O'Hagan. A lawyer, yet. Can this be true. If they all look like you in that great city, I must come up there and get myself in some trouble.'

They were an instant success with each other. Abigail said—

'If I'd known Mark was going to bring me to your famous restaurant, I wouldn't have let him fill me full of dinner elsewhere. Shame on you Mark.'

The injustice of it was so enormous that I just stood there, fish-eyed. Krantz tutted.

'You never know who your friends are in this town,' he said darkly. 'Well, don't worry Miss O'Hagan. You must come again, as my guest. And soon.'

He went back to the revolving leather chair and sat down.

'Well now, Preston, it's been a long time. You didn't come here to eat, not even with this lovely lawyer here, so you want something. What?'

51

'The Bear-Bear Club,' I opened. 'Does it mean anything?'

He shook his head.

'Not right off the top. New place, huh?'

'Very new,' I agreed. 'Only been open a week or two. It's where the Old Log Cabin used to be.'

That brought a better reaction.

'Ah yes. That one I know. Out by the lake, someplace. The Davis brothers' place. They been having a lot of bad luck the last year or two. Finally decided to cash up and buy a fishing boat. They were getting on in years, anyway.'

I lit an Old Favorite, and pulled a floor ashtray closer to hand.

'It's the new owners I'm interested in. You wouldn't happen to know who they are, huh?'

He shrugged.

'Not these days. I don't really keep in touch any more. Did you think of asking Lennard?'

I'd thought about it, and dismissed it. Tom Lennard was not a man I would want to approach in the ordinary way, particularly if I could get what I wanted from Krantz.

'Leonard who?' queried Abigail.

I shot her a baleful glance, but Ben was all smiles.

'That's his last name, Lennard,' he explained. 'Tom Lennard. He has a lot to do with new businesses opening around this area. Imagine, you being a lawyer. You don't look old enough.'

Abigail made a face.

'The good people of San Francisco would agree with that. It's tough enough just being a woman lawyer. To be young into the bargain makes it almost a crime.'

Krantz's eyes twinkled.

'Rough going, huh? Well one favor deserves another. How would it be if I spoke to one or two people? I have some close friends up there, and I'm sure they could put a little business your way.'

She was pleased as punch. As well she might be. A word from Reuben Krantz was in the nature of a royal request, though Abigail had no way of knowing it.

'Why, that's extremely generous of you Mr. Krantz.'

'Call me Ben. Please.'

'Ben then. But you said something about returning a favor. What did I ever do for you?'

He smiled, with genuine pleasure.

'You came into my place, didn't you?'

They beamed at each other in mutual esteem. It was sickening.

'How's the indigestion these days, Ben?'

That ought to break it up. Krantz suffers from some mysterious gastric ailment, which no doctor seems able to diagnose. He spends a fortune on remedies and consultations, with no lasting effects. Now, he looked at me reproachfully.

'At the moment, it's what those doctors call quiescent. That is to say, it isn't actually giving me any discomfort, but it's just resting down there.'

'What happened about that seaweed formula you were going to try?'

He shrugged.

'It seemed to work for a couple of days, until the system worked out a counter-attack. Then we were back to normal.'

If I'd thought to deter Miss Fixit by drawing attention to Ben Krantz' frailties, I'd got the wrong girl. She was all sympathetic concern.

'What's he talking about, Ben? Is this some kind of indigestion?'

'Not exactly. Most of the doctors start off thinking that way. Then, when they really look into it—'

We got a rundown on what happened when the doctors really looked into it. Or rather, Abigail did. I'd heard it all before. They went on, really looking into it, for the best part of ten minutes, while I sat there inspecting my shoes. They clashed with the carpet.

'You know,' said Doctor O'Hagan finally, 'this sounds very much like what happened to my cousin Charlie. Same old symptoms, same traipsing around from one doctor to another.'

'He has my sympathy,' nodded Krantz.

'But he got cured in the end. About two years ago. He went to some new place, and they fixed him up within a month.'

A gleaming silver pencil appeared in the listener's hand, as if by magic.

'The details, if you please.'

Abigail shook her head.

'I'm sorry. You'll think I'm terrible, but I didn't follow it all that closely. I was just glad he got better, and thought no more about it.'

The pencil wavered sadly, then lay down on the table.

'Quite understandable. If you should ever run into your cousin—'

'Oh, don't you worry. I'll be on the telephone, first thing tomorrow, and let you have the whole story.'

Ben had been going to stand her to dinner, just for the favor of her presence. If she cured his stomach complaint, he'd probably hand over the deeds of the Cloister.

'If it was anything else,' he assured her, 'I would say, please don't trouble. But in this case, please take as much trouble as you can.'

The good doctor smiled warmly.

'Leave it to me. I'd phone him now, if it wasn't so late.'

'Please.' He held up a hand. 'I've had this for so long now, one more day is bearable.'

I'd had more than enough of both of them. I stood up.

'Well, nice to see you Ben. We must be getting along.'

His reception of that was less friendly.

'Next time you must make it a real visit,' he

said frostily. But there was no frost when he looked back at her. 'I'll be looking forward to your call.'

'Some time tomorrow,' she promised.

The creep even kissed her hand, and she showed every sign of enjoying it. The royal progress continued all the way to the car, with Biff bobbing and smiling every inch of the way.

'What nice people,' she declared with smug satisfaction, as we pulled away.

'They were just softening you up,' I sneered. 'You ought to fetch a good price. Krantz is a white slaver, really. The chophouse is just a front.'

She had one kind of laugh which was a small tinkly sound. That was the one she gave me then.

'My my,' she remonstrated. 'We wouldn't be a teeny bit jealous, would we?'

'What about?' I retorted. 'You're not the only seventy-year-old dame in this town. I could call up a dozen or more, right now.'

She pouted, and moved a whole inch away from me.

'I imagine. Old school friends, I expect. Where are we going now? What about this man Lennard? Too late to see him, I suppose?'

I'd been wondering about that while she and Krantz were touching toes. It certainly was not too late to go looking for Tom Lennard, but I didn't know exactly where I'd find him at that hour of night. Wherever it was, one thing was clear, it was no place for a lady.

'It's pretty late,' I agreed. 'He can wait till tomorrow.'

'Who is he, anyway? Why might he be able to help?'

'That's hard to put over,' I said cagily. 'I suppose you might describe him as a kind of unofficial labor organiser in the catering business. Any place that employs waiters, cooks, hotel maids, all those kinds of people, has to have the nod from Lennard.'

'The nod,' she repeated. 'That's some kind of slang isn't it? Sounds like approval, or acquiescence, am I right?'

I swerved out of the path of some lunatic, and said a word or two about him.

'On the button,' I replied, eventually. 'He has to say O.K. before the doors can open.'

'But you said he was unofficial,' she demurred. 'Surely the proper labor people are the ones with the influence about things like that?'

I smiled, without humor.

'Oh sure, when it comes to the rate for the job, and all that kind of stuff. But unless Lennard says so, places can't run.'

'You're speaking of intimidation. That can't still happen?'

'Not the way it used to,' I told her. 'If you're thinking in terms of bombs being tossed around, people getting beaten up, no. That's

57

out, mostly. Today we have sophistication in this field, just like in others. Food deliveries don't arrive on time, key people don't turn up for work, mysterious power failures happen. There are all kinds of ways of stopping a place from operating. Most of them are unpredictable. Untraceable, too. But the effect is the same.'

To do her credit, she heard me through to the end, without interruption. Then she weighed in.

'But this is monstrous. This is the eighties, not the twenties. The way you and Ben Krantz talked about this man makes it obvious that everybody knows about him. Why isn't something done?'

'And you a lawyer too,' I reproved. 'You should know better. Knowing isn't proving. Not in a courtroom. Certainly, everybody knows. Certainly the lawboys will be watching him, you can bet on that. But they have to have a lot of hard, irrefutable facts before they dare go to law. Those facts can be hard to come by, when you're dealing with a man like Tom Lennard.'

She wasn't satisfied, but evidently decided to drop the matter. For the time being, at least.

'Well, let's leave that. Our immediate concern is the Bear-Bear Club. If I understand you correctly, you're saying that this Mr. Lennard will have been involved with the new management at some stage or other. Therefore, he'll be in a position to tell us more

58

about them.'

'That's about it,' I agreed. 'Except that I didn't say "us". This man can be very rough company.'

'Oh, you,' she sniffed, and said nothing further all the way back.

There was another problem playing on my mind, and it was far removed from the theoretical constructions to be put on Joseph P. McEvoy's absence. This was presence. It was now into the small hours of the morning, and there couldn't be any question of fixing her up with a hotel.

We were both busy with our private thoughts when I opened up the door of the apartment, and stood back to let her in. She went inside slowly, trailing her coat along the ground by one hand.

'It's pretty late,' I began.

'Yes, I know. I'd like some coffee, if you don't mind.'

'Sure. You know where everything is. Do you mind?'

She went off into the kitchen, and made coffee noises. I sat down, to light a cigaret and think.

The telephone rang. When I picked it up, a man's voice said—

'Is that a Mr. Mark Preston?'

The voice was low-pitched, gravelly, and unfamiliar.

'I'm Preston,' I confirmed. 'Who is this?'

'I'll get to it,' he stalled. 'You're Preston the P.I., right?'

'Right.'

'And you're asking around about this dame, this Sally Dewes?'

The conversation was showing promise. Abigail stuck her head through the open kitchen door and frowned enquiringly. I beckoned her over, and put my finger to my lips for silence.

'If you know anything about Miss Dewes, I might be interested,' I offered cautiously.

'Like ten bucks interested?' he pressed.

'I might go to ten for good merchandise. What are you selling?'

Abigail wanted to butt in, but I shook my head fiercely.

'I'm selling the address. I know where she lives.'

'O.K. Shoot.'

His tone changed, and a whining protest came into it.

'Aw now, c'm on Mr. Preston. I tell you what I know, and you forget about the tenspot, am I right?'

'You'll get your money if the information is good,' I said impatiently.

'Bring it to me,' he returned. 'I'm in a joint called the Round-Up. It's in Crane Street. You know it?'

'I can find it. What's your name?'

'Briggs. I'm Bosun Briggs.'

Sounded like a seafaring man, and Crane Street is close to the waterfront.

'How long will you be there?'

'Until you show. I don't have no garden parties to attend.'

'Give me about twenty minutes, Briggs.'

I put down the phone, wondering. Abigail handed over coffee and I took it with nodded thanks.

'Are we going out again?' she asked brightly.

'No. We are not going anywhere. I am going down to some joint on the waterfront. Even the waterfront dames keep away from the Round-Up, leave alone anyone like you.'

She scowled.

'What do I do? I didn't bring my embroidery.'

'You'd better make up some kind of bed on the couch, then get yourself into the bedroom. I'll sleep out here when I get back. Oh, and lock your door. I'm not so sure I trust myself around you.'

That seemed to cheer her up.

'Well good. I was beginning to think my moustache was putting you off.'

I got up, and we grinned. I was thinking Bosun Briggs had probably deferred some kind of a decision.

There was no way I could tell what Abigail was thinking, but she was looking decidedly thoughtful as I closed the door.

# FIVE

Say what you like about Conquest Street, at least it starts out in the right spirit, and then deteriorates. Crane Street doesn't even make that little pretense. It starts out with high level deterioration and maintains that lofty standard throughout its length. An area where you say a prayer each time you leave your car, and on two counts. In the first place, you hope you're going to be able to get back to it, what with all the mug artists and all. In the second place, assuming you get back to it, you hope it's going to be there to get back to. If you see what I mean.

The Round-Up is a two-storey wooden frame with heavy shutters over the windows at all times. Seems to me a builder would save money by leaving out the windows in the first place. Chinks of yellow light escaped thankfully from the occasional crack in the shutters, otherwise there was no way of telling the joint was open. I pushed open the doors and went in. The whole floor was just one big bar, with the bare minimum of wooden furniture scattered around the sawdust floor. The management evidently did not believe in increasing the overheads by putting on a big front. The light-fittings, too, were early-Barbary. Plain lengths of cable dangling starkly from the ceiling, with one fly-specked lamp per dangle. The far wall consisted of one long bar, behind which two gorillas were stationed. They would serve beer, mop up, or bend a skull, according to need, and it showed.

The clientele was the same distinguished crowd of jet-setters you would find in any waterfront bar, anywhere in the world, at two thirty in the ack emma. The fact that my jacket matched my pants made me stand out like a darn on a pool-table. One or two of the customers nudged each other, and eyed me, as I walked across to the bar. I was thankful for the confidence radiating from the hard metal of the thirty-eight, pushing against my middle.

One of the tame gorillas squinted at me from folded eyelids.

'You want what?'

He didn't like me, and he wasn't about to make any bones about it.

'Looking for a man,' I replied easily, leaning on the bar.

'Ours are all taken,' he said nastily. 'So blow.'

'S'O.K. Swede. We got a little business.'

I turned to inspect the newcomer. He was thirty-five, pale-faced, unhealthy looking. Too fat for his height, which was around five seven. Already, I knew one thing about Bosun Briggs. It had been a long time since he went to sea, if ever. He wore a greasy sweat shirt, which could have been yellow at some time, with a picture of a red-eyed bull stamped on it.

'You the man who called me?' I queried.

'Right. Why don't you spring a couple beers, and we'll go into my private office?'

I indicated two bottles where the labels were recognisable. The formidable Swede banged them down in front of me.

'Do you break tops in this hotel?'

I pointed to the pressed metal caps. He glowered, then produced an opener and ripped off the caps.

'I do teeth also,' he informed me.

'I can imagine.'

Briggs picked up his beer, and motioned me to follow him. Nobody said anything about glasses. He went over to an empty table, and waved a hand.

'C'm on in. Cosy, huh.'

'Bit overfurnished for my taste,' I replied.

I sat in a chair backing onto the wall. That gave me an all-round view in case anyone felt like coming up and passing the time of day. Briggs noted this, and chuckled. He had a breath like a deceased crocodile.

'You ain't a very trusting fellow, huh?'

'I like a nice view of the sea,' I told him.

'Now then, let's get down to cases. What made you call me?'

He put on a look of cunning which didn't improve his general attraction.

'Did you bring the dough?'

'First things first. Why'd you call me?'

'Somebody said you was trying to find this dame. I knew where to look. Seemed to me we ought to get together in the cash department.'

I sighed impatiently.

'I already figured that for myself. I want to know who it was told you. This is kind of confidential business. It makes me nervous when every little wharf-rat starts muscling in.'

His face darkened.

'Who you calling names? Listen, you don't come down here shooting off your mouth that way. This here's my territory. You wanta know something? There's people here that'll tear off your ears, just for laughs. It wouldn't be no sweat to take you for everything on you, and still tell you nothing.' He took a swig at his bottle. 'You watch your mouth, or maybe I'll tell 'em to do just that. Maybe I will, anyway.'

I looked around. There were seven other customers in the place, and there was nothing magnificent about them.

'Now hear this,' I advised him. 'You are out of your league, Briggs. You and all this scum. You tell me what I want to hear, and maybe I'll give you the ten. But any more of the fancy chatter, and I'll smear you all over the walls. And your little friends, too. See what I mean?'

I opened my coat, and eased the thirty-eight into plain view, but where only my new friend could see it. His jaw dropped.

'Listen, there's no need for none of that stuff,' he stammered. 'I come in here fair and square—'

'And you can go out the same way, if you come across with the goods. Now, let's start over. How did you know I was in the market?'

He heaved his shoulders resignedly.

'What's the harm? My sister told me.'

'Sister? Where does she come into this?'

'From the club,' he explained, as though it was perfectly obvious. 'You was out there tonight, asking about the Dewes dame.'

I thought back over my visit to the Bear-Bear Club. The only woman I'd had any kind of contact with had been the blonde juggler.

'Does she do an act out there?' I demanded.

'You got it,' he agreed proudly. 'Lolita Montez, the juggler, that's my sister.'

It still made no sense.

'But I didn't speak to her,' I protested.

'It's this way,' he explained, 'the kid is kind of stuck on a guy out there. Name of Jack Durrant. And don't say you never talked to him, 'cause I know different.'

'Yeah, I talked with Durrant. So your little sister was listening?'

'Right. She thought you looked like trouble, so she'd better cop an earful, so she could yell for the cavalry if you got out of line.'

'I wondered how the bouncer turned up so fast. But that doesn't tell me why she called you. If she's hot for this Durrant, why should she help me? Or, if she wanted to, why not tell me herself?'

Briggs spread his hands.

'Listen, the day I understand dames will be like a turning point in my life. Durrant is shacked up with this one you want, this Dewes. Betty don't like it—that's her real name, Betty, not Lolita—'

'Do tell—' I said, all surprised—

'—so she figures maybe the dame is in trouble, and you're the trouble. Naturally, she can't put you two in the same room fast enough. At the same time, she don't want to be the one who blows the whistle, because that could put her in bad with Durrant. So she figures it out. She gets me to point the finger. I make a little dough, Betty stays in the clear, and this Dewes collects any trouble you're handing out. Neat, huh?'

'You're a lovely family,' I assured him. 'It must make the old folks very proud.'

'Well, never mind the dirty cracks. You want the rest of it, or not?'

'I want it.'

Since I knew before I entered the place just what kind of joint the Round-Up was, I had slipped the money out of my wallet before I went in there. It was no place to be waving leather. Now, I lifted out a crumpled bill and placed it on the table. Briggs' eyes glistened briefly.

'The Maybelle Apartments. Number sixteen twenty-two.'

'You're sure about this? I'd hate to have to

come back down here and beat this out of you.'

'Why would I give you a dumb lead?' he queried. 'I got nothing to gain. This Dewes is nothing in my life.'

It was probably true. I stood up.

'The money stays. You too. I don't care for the thought of a thing like you being behind me out there.'

Two or three of the barflies showed signs of interest in my coming departure. This wasn't lost on Briggs, who seemed to regain some of his confidence. Picking up the ten, he shoved it into a pocket.

'I'm staying right here,' he assured me. 'What other people do is no concern of mine.'

Every eye in the place was boring into my back as I strode across the room and out into the night. I was intending to sprint the few yards to the car, and get it unlocked, before the committee turned out to give me a rousing send-off. But once I hit the street, I realised there was no hurry. A police cruiser was parked in front of me, two uniformed officers leaning on their own roof, and waiting.

'This your car?'

There was no friendliness in the voice that cut through the night. Nothing but suspicion, and hostility.

'Yes, it is.'

'Get over here and spread 'em out.'

The barking voice didn't even explain what

that meant. It was assumed that anybody prowling around Crane Street at three in the morning would be familiar with police procedure. It was galling to have to prove him right. Bearing in mind the hour and the place, I made no attempt to be awkward. Walking to the cruiser, I pressed myself against it, stretching my arms out flat on the roof, head ditto.

'A wise guy,' grumbled One. 'He didn't even argue.'

'Probably just a collector for a hospital charity,' grated Two. 'We get 'em down here all the time.'

Hard hands moved over me. It didn't take long to locate the gun.

'Hey, this guy has a piece.'

'No kidding. Think he'd mind if we had a look at it?'

The gun slid away, and my middle felt lonely.

'All right you, turn around. Let's see your identification.'

'Inside pocket, top left,' I told him.

'Take it out.'

I didn't like these two. I didn't like the look of them or the sound of them, and I was miles out of my neighborhood.

'You take it out,' I replied evenly. 'I wouldn't want to get shot by accident because you thought I was pulling a weapon on you.'

'Don't you sass me, animal. I might just

wipe you across the face with this.'

'This' was a blue-black Police Special, and it looked enormous in that calloused fist. There was a wicked grin on the face hovering in the air a few feet from me. I could and would raise hell if this character did me any damage, but that wouldn't repair the damage.

'All right,' I tried to sound authoritative, 'that's enough. Call Captain John Rourke of Homicide.'

The face looked puzzled.

'Rourke? You know Rourke?'

'Just call him.'

Instead, he pushed a hard hand inside my jacket, and pulled out my leather. The other man called over—

'What've you got, Ed?'

Ed held the open wallet down, so that the light from inside the car hit it.

'Hey, what do you know. A private badge. We got us a real live Sam Spade. If he didn't steal the I .D., that is. Did you?'

'My picture is there. All you have to do is look.'

'This thing?' He stabbed scornfully at the small shiny square. 'Listen, this could be anybody, from Mickey Mouse on.'

I keep meaning to get that damned picture changed.

'If you're not satisfied, call Rourke,' I said wearily.

He still didn't like me.

'Anybody can say that,' he scoffed. 'Anybody would know the captain is likely home in bed at three in the morning.'

I shrugged.

'It makes no difference. Somebody is always on duty at Homicide. Whoever it is will know me. Randall will be there, or Schulz.'

The second patrolman came closer and peered at me.

'You really know all those guys?'

For once in my life I was thankful it was true.

'We're like one big family,' I assured him. 'Check it.

'Seems like I seen you before,' he said doubtfully. Then turning to his partner, he asked, 'What's the name in there?'

'Preston.'

'Yeah. I gotcha. Preston, that's it. He's O.K. Ed, I remember him.'

But Ed was reluctant to let it go.

'So what's a bigshot P.I. doing down in this neck of the woods, at this goddamned hour of the morning? This isn't exactly millionaire country, right?'

'Right,' I agreed. 'I wanted to talk to a man. That doesn't break any statutes, not even in this precinct.'

'What man?'

I shook my head.

'Call Rourke,' I said again.

'I don't like you, Preston,' he snapped

vindictively.

But the conviction was lacking now, and in fact he was losing confidence. I was regaining mine. The worst was over.

'That's a shame, Ed. I've taken quite a shine to you. Matter of fact, I was thinking of mentioning you to the City Ombudsman.'

The wallet was shoved back at me then.

'Just drive,' he hissed. 'Get in the car and drive.'

I stood upright, smoothing at my crumpled jacket.

'I'll take the iron,' I said, holding out a hand.

We both stayed immobile for a few seconds, glaring at each other.

'Give it to him Ed,' prompted my benefactor. 'There's nothing here for us.'

'I wouldn't be too sure about that,' I contradicted. 'Looks as though the club members are turning out to give you boys a welcome.'

Behind them the door of the Round-Up stood open, and a clutch of faces were rubbernecking at the free show.

'Get back in there, there's nothing to see,' shouted Two. Then turning to me he added, 'That includes you, Preston. Don't push your luck.'

With the gun back in place, I walked quickly to my own car, climbed in and drove away.

*　　*　　*

It's an odd feeling, trying not to make any noise letting yourself into your own apartment.

The lights were out, except for one table lamp in the corner, which enabled me to make it across the room without falling over any furniture. I tiptoed over to the chesterfield, and peeked down. The sheets were rumpled, ditto the pillow, but there was no Abigail. Where her head should have been was a large piece of paper, with something written on it. I picked this up, and moved nearer to the light. It said, in one-inch capitals—

THIS IS LUMPY. I'M IN THE BEDROOM. H'm.

I was pretty tired by now, but this latest development meant that before I got any sleep, I was going to have to hold a meeting. With myself.

There was cold coffee in the kitchen. I slopped some into a beaker, and added a small measure of scotch, to take off the chill. Then I lit an Old Favorite, and sat down, as far from the empty couch as I could get.

What did she mean, lumpy?

I've had to sleep on the thing myself, the odd occasion in the past. I never found it particularly lumpy. In fact, as shakedowns go, it was as comfortable a sleep as I've had anywhere.

And what did she mean 'I'm in the bedroom?'

73

Did she mean 'I'm in the bedroom, so you may take this as notice that the place is occupied?'

Or did she mean 'I'm in the bedroom, so you'll know where to find me?'

Taking the first alternative, now that would be pretty cool, the way I saw it. That would be the same as saying 'this chesterfield is not good enough for me, so I'm taking the bed. You can have the lumps.' Which, considering it's my apartment, is kind of a high-handed attitude, by anybody's standards. But then, I reminded myself, I was dealing with Abigail H. O'Hagan, who could be described as kind of high-handed, on occasions.

There was always the second alternative. She could be saying 'nobody can sleep on those lumps, so we'll just have to share the bed.' She could be saying that, I admitted. Which again, would come into the cool category. The idea of sharing a bed with Abigail was by no means the most repugnant prospect I could think of, but I would have preferred to have had a more dominant role in the taking of that particular decision. This way, it just didn't feel right. It almost put me in the position of making the girl pay for her room and board. And if you think that's a prudish kind of attitude for me to be taking, let me remind you it wasn't you sitting there at four in the morning, and this wasn't just any dame.

This was Abigail.

I stared into the bottom of the coffee cup. If I wasn't intending to spend the rest of the night drinking, this was decision time.

Blast Abigail.

Blast Joseph P. McEvoy, wherever he may be. He got me into this.

Blast the entire man/woman set-up.

Maybe I made the wrong decision. It's easy to do when you're worn out.

I couldn't find any lumps.

# SIX

Some day I'm going to get a quieter door buzzer installed. This present one sounds like an electric buzz saw. Mumbling and stumbling, I was halfway to the door when the fog cleared, and I remembered what the current situation was. It was also coming through the haze that I ought to be wondering who it was at the door at—let's see—eight thirty in the morning.

Well, there's only one way to resolve that particular difficulty. I peered through the spy-hole, at a large, familiar, and unwelcome face.

'Peek-a-boo,' said Randall.

I groaned, noted that I'd failed to lock up properly the previous night, and opened the door. Detective Sergeant Gil Randall of Homicide beamed at me.

75

'I was just in the neighbourhood,' he greeted. 'Thought we might catch up on old times.'

I hesitated, because of Abigail. I wanted to give her whatever protection I could, though Heaven knows, nobody ever showed less need of it.

'You didn't say "come in",' my visitor pointed out.

'Oh sure, sure. Come on in Gil. I'm still half asleep.'

'Oh tut tut, did I disturb you?' he said unfeelingly. 'It's just that when you're a flatfoot you forget there are people in the world who sometimes spend hours on end in bed.'

He moved massively inside, half-filling the place with his enormous bulk. With his craggy face and heavy-lidded eyes, Randall gives an impression of slowness in every department. People can tell just by looking at him that he's not quick in the think-box. They can also see for themselves that the man is a ponderous mover, and unlikely to cause any problems in the speedy area. That's what people can tell, and you can find any number of such people, at any convenient time. All you have to do is take a ride out to the state penitentiary, which owes a lot of its custom to old slow-thinking, sluggish-moving Randall.

Well, this wasn't my first sight of him, and he didn't fool me. The guy has a mind like a rapier, and when fast physical movement is on the agenda, he's just a little faster than an irritable rattlesnake. And just as deadly.

Already he'd summed up the sleeping set-up.

'Times are hard, huh?'

'Hard?'

I was looking around for my shoes. He nodded, settling himself comfortably into a chair.

'I would say hard, when a man has to hock his bed. Or am I jumping to conclusions?'

I managed to assume my eight thirty a.m. caricature of a grin.

'Oh, that. No. My cousin has been visiting.'

'Cousin?'

'Yeah, my cousin from Chattanooga.'

I hoped my dear cousin would have the sense to stay in the bedroom. Always assuming she was awake, that is.

'No kidding? Like in the Choo Choo? I never met anybody who's really been there before.'

And if I was lucky, he wasn't about to.

'Well now, nice of you to drop in, and all that stuff, but to what do I owe the pleasure?'

'That's the trouble with you get-up-and-go characters,' he grumbled. 'Always wanting to hit that ball. Some places I go, they put on the coffee pot first.'

Well, if his visit was that friendly, I ought to be grateful. It wasn't his fault I had this human bombshell tucked away in the bedroom.

'Coming up.'

I went out to set up the brew, returning quickly, so that he couldn't start roaming around, opening doors. He wrinkled his nose, and the eyes either side of it were no more than slits.

'That's some pretty fancy shaving lotion they use over there in Chattanooga,' he observed drily.

Abigail's perfume was already so much a part of the atmosphere that it hadn't registered this morning. Not with me, that is.

'Ah, there it is.'

I ignored the comment, making a great show of recovering my beaker from where I'd dumped it the night before. The morning before. Well, er, four hours earlier. Then I went back to my kitchen duties, and came out with the steaming drinks.

'Doesn't your cousin get any?'

'I'm not running a hotel,' I replied grumpily. 'Now then, you've got your coffee. Let's get to it.'

He sipped, and nodded approval.

'Not half bad,' he acknowledged. 'Just left some people, we were chattering around this and that. Your name came up.'

I heard this without pleasure.

'It happens,' I shrugged. 'I'm kind of a popular figure in some quarters.'

'Really? Not in these quarters, you ain't.

Oh, come to think of it, you did have one friend there.'

'Well, there you are. I have so many friends. Which particular one are we talking about?'

'Name of Briggs,' his eyes never left my face. 'You're not going to tell me you don't know him?'

I looked like a man trying to concentrate on the name Briggs.

'Briggs, Briggs,' I muttered. 'Can't seem to bring him back.'

'Try harder,' he advised sourly. 'You were with him not so many hours ago.'

'Is that what he says?' I countered.

'That's what I say,' he emphasised. 'That's also what eight independent witnesses say. You want to make liars out of all those people?'

With such a crowd involved, he could only be talking about the distinguished patrons of the Round-Up on Crane Street.

'And what does he say?' I challenged. 'My dear old buddy, Briggs?'

'No comment,' returned Randall. 'He's all through making comments. You said just now you couldn't bring him back. Neither could the medics. Something about his breathing problems, with those three slugs in his lungs.'

So somebody had killed him. That was bad. Bad for me, because I must have been one of the last people to see him alive.

'Ah,' I said.

As a comment, it didn't get the discussion

very much further forward.

'That's it?' queried Randall, astonished. ' "Ah"? Just "ah"? You wouldn't care to elaborate on that, just a little bit?'

'Well, it's quite a shock, you must admit,' I replied. 'Poor old Briggs, dead like that. Who would have done such a thing?'

It was his turn to say 'ah'.

'Ah.' He wagged a finger the size of a sausage.

'You may well ask. Oddly enough, other people are asking the same thing. I'm one of them. Wondered whether you might have any thoughts about it?'

He didn't think I'd been responsible for Bosun Briggs' death. That much was obvious. The conversation would have taken a very different turn, if he had. But, just the same, he was going to want some answers. I would have to watch my tongue, if I was going to keep Abigail out of all this. What she and her dear old pappy were doing, in trying to find McEvoy without reporting the offense, could be categorised as concealment of a felony, if some bad-tempered policeman wanted to call it that.

'Well now,' I stalled. 'I'm trying to think. Like to help if I can.'

That brought me a snort of some dimensions.

'I'm sure you would. Think back to what you talked with him about. It's somewhere to start.'

Briggs was dead. If he'd been able to make any dying statements, they would not have involved me. What a dying man does is to put the finger on whoever killed him. Therefore, it was a reasonable assumption that the only person left who knew about our conversation, was me.

'O.K.,' I said, all helpful. 'I got this call—'

'—time?'

'Oh. One thirty. Two o'clock. It was this man Briggs. I'd never met the guy, never even heard of him before, but he wanted to see me. He said certain parties might be willing to cooperate in that Prentice Watch Company heist.'

'Cooperate how?'

I looked pained. Randall knew as well as I did how these things worked. The thieves make off with somebody else's property. Then, if the insurance reward is attractive enough, they negotiate the return of the stuff through some third party, no questions asked. Everybody is satisfied, except the police, because when it's all over, no doors slam. The Prentice robbery had only taken place a couple of days earlier, so it would not be unreasonable for a deal of this kind to be sounded out.

'Come on Gil,' I chaffed, 'you know how it works. Anyway, I didn't think it would do any harm to talk to the guy. I went down to this terrible joint on Crane Street—'

'We know where you went,' he interrupted. 'The point is, did you make a deal?'

'No,' I denied. 'No deal. I think Briggs was bluffing. He wasn't one of the guys who actually took part, if I was to believe him. All he had was some information about who was responsible. He wanted to set up a deal with me, so that he could contact the people who had the stuff, and cut himself in for a piece of the action.'

'That's against the law,' said my visitor heavily.

'Just what I told him,' I replied blandly. 'And in any case, I don't make deals with middlemen. I told him I might listen if I was talking to one of the principals, but only then.'

'That's still against the law.'

He was being very difficult today.

'Only if you do it,' I corrected. 'All I did was talk about it.'

'H'm. Do you still have the same thirty-eight you had last time we checked?'

'Yes. You want to see it?'

A huge paw waved.

'Nah. What's the point? This Briggs was killed with a thirty-eight, but if you'd done that, you wouldn't be so dumb as to use a weapon on which we have thorough documentation.'

There was something here I didn't understand. It wasn't simply that Randall didn't think I'd killed Briggs. It was more than

82

that. He knew perfectly well it wasn't me. The point was, how did he know? What made him so certain?

'I'm sorry I can't be more helpful,' I assured him. 'Fact is, I didn't really know the guy at all. Just a man in a bar.'

He heaved himself to his feet, grunting.

'As it happens, I'm going to believe you, but don't get too grateful. There are two guys down in that precinct house who don't like you. They called me up, because you tossed my name around down there last night. So I said I'd just walk through the part with you, see if you had anything. Now, I'm going to tell them no. But it might not end there. This isn't my squeal, not yet, and they may still haul you in just for laughs. Especially one of 'em.'

'Name of Ed something?'

'Think it was. What did you do to him?'

I shook my head.

'Nothing. That's the truth. The guy got sore because he had me all worked out as some kind of hood. What with the wheels, and the suit and everything, I didn't have any business to be in such a neighborhood at such an hour. That's all it was. I was a disappointment.'

Randall walked to the door.

'I know how he feels. You've been a disappointment to me before now. Listen, about this Prentice job. You hear any more about it, I recommend you to get in touch with the Loft Squad. You wouldn't want to go

83

each other.

'You remember I said I had to go and meet a man last night?'

'Of course.'

'It was a waterfront place, and you can paint your own picture of what that means. This man fitted in there like part of the furniture. Only there wasn't any. Furniture, that is. We talked, and when I left, one or two of the local hooray brigade were all set to come after me. In a way, I was lucky. The law was waiting outside for me. They asked me a few questions, then let me go.'

Her face was puzzled.

'You know how this is coming over, do you?'

'Tell me.'

She bit her lip.

'I don't want to hurt your feelings, Mark, but this sounds like a man trying to impress a simple girl with what a tough character he is. Out there in the night, risking life and limb, and all for the love etc. etc. In short, it sounds like showing off, and I don't get it. It isn't like you at all.'

I sighed. Maybe it did sound that way, but I had to go on with it. Somehow or other, this girl had to be made to understand the seriousness of things.

'That is not the idea. I'm trying to tell you that things have changed. While we were looking for your friend McEvoy, it wasn't so bad. From what you say about the man, and

86

from what I know about cases like this, we had a reasonable chance of locating him. He'd be shacked up somewhere with Sally Dewes, living the life of Riley, and wondering if he'd be able to spend all the money before he got caught. I've seen dozens like him. Not bad men, not really bad. Just chumps, who got pushed off center by a pretty face. When they're caught, and they always are, they just shrug their shoulders and give up. Things are different now. The nasty people have started to crawl out of the woodwork. I want you out of it.'

I waited for the arguments, keeping my sucker punch for the end. There wasn't long to wait.

'You can't be serious,' she protested. Then, seeing my face, 'You are serious. Well, I've heard nothing yet to convince me. And what do you mean, out of it? This is my case, Preston. You're kind of a Johnny-come-lately here. What did he say to you, this character last night? Seems to have scared the pants off you. Not a pretty sight.'

If I let her make me mad, I would lose ground. Keeping my tone even, I replied—

'I'm trying to explain to you that the Junior G-Girl bit is out. It was O.K. for a while, and maybe we both enjoyed it, but from this point on, you have to let me handle things. Otherwise—'

I left the threat unfinished.

'Otherwise what?' she queried nastily. 'Don't you threaten me. I don't threaten too well.'

'Otherwise I may drop it altogether,' I finished.

She clenched her hands, in impotent rage.

'Well now, you listen, while I tell you how all this sounds from where I'm sitting. It sounds to me like you didn't mind coming along for the ride, so long as it was a simple matter of tracking down Joe McEvoy, and sharing half the profits. Now that things are beginning to look nasty, you want to chicken out. All this hoohah about protecting me, is for the birds. You know I wouldn't stand for it, and that gives you your ticket out. That's exactly how it sounds to me. And you still haven't told me what the nasty man said to frighten you.'

It was getting increasingly difficult to restrain my temper.

'Think whatever you will. This is no place for you any more. You think you can handle yourself, O'Hagan, and up to a point you're right. The point has now been passed. The guy I saw last night was named Briggs. Does it mean anything?'

'Briggs? No. Not to me. What about him?'

'This about him. He told me where to find Sally Dewes. It was too late for me to follow it up, but I'll do it today. Other people knew he'd been talking to me, and one of them didn't like it. Just to emphasise the point, this somebody put three bullets into his chest. He's down at the city morgue, with a piece of card tied to his big toe. That's why the police were here this morning. Some of them would like to pin the murder on me. Am I getting through at last?'

The question was unnecessary. Her face had already told me the answer.

'I—I don't know what to say,' she faltered. 'You make me feel terrible.'

'Good,' I told her remorselessly. 'You have every right. At least now you can understand why I want you where it's warm and safe. What's it going to be?'

The tawny head was lowered, as she studied her hands.

'I feel terrible.'

'You already said that. And I said "good".'

'How could I talk to you that way? How could I have thought—?'

Don't kick a man when he's down. That's the rule. At last, that's the rule when the man is a woman.

'It's all right, Abigail. See—no broken bones. Do we have a deal?'

She nodded tremulously.

'I guess we do. Mind you, I'm not out of it entirely. But you call the shots. Yes?'

It would have to do for a start.

'Right. Now let's put it out of our heads for now. Was something said about breakfast?'

'Coming up.'

# SEVEN

The Maybelle Apartments is one of those places which is neither up nor down in the social scale. It's what you might classify as a residential departure platform. For people on the way up, the Maybelle would be the first step away from the ground level, a jumping-off place. For those on the way down, it would be the last stage before the big obscurity.

It was a little past noon when I got there, and the sun was bouncing off everything it could find. Any sensible man would be in a nice cool bar, preferably with a beach view, not walking around in the heat like some people. The numbering system for the apartments was original, to put it kindly, but I finally located 1622 on the fourth floor of the fourth block. There was no name-card outside, and no noise from inside when I leaned on the bell.

After a while I could hear movement from the other side of the door. A bolt scraped and I was looking at an eye, which was accompanied by a female voice.

'Yes?'

'Sally Dewes? I'd like to talk with you, please.'

'Go away. There's nobody here by that name.'

'I'll be back in ten minutes. With the police.'

The door was almost closed when I said it. Now it paused.

'Police? What would they want with me?'

'If you let me in, I'll explain all that.'

'Who are you?'

She was a little late, remembering to ask that one. It was almost as if she knew who I would be.

'Name of Preston. Here.'

I held out that thing again, but this time there was no crack about the photograph. Instead, a chain slid and the door was opened.

'I guess it's all right.'

Stepping inside, I got a look at the tenant. She was under thirty in the years department, well over thirty in other areas. Beneath the fringe-cut blonde head was a knowing face.

'All right, so you're in. What do you want? By the way, let me show you a photograph.'

She pointed to the wall. There was a picture of her in a sweat suit, holding a cup and smiling at the camera.

'Dominoes?' I queried.

'Karate,' she corrected. 'Just so there's no misunderstanding.'

I grinned.

'Look, Miss Dewes, or is it Mrs?'

'It isn't Dewes at all. What's this all about?'

By way of answer I asked—

'Is Durrant here?'

'No, he's—'

She stopped talking almost at once, but it

was too late.

'Well, never mind,' I said heartily, 'we can manage without him. Why don't I just call you Sally, to save all this pussyfooting around?'

That brought me a shrug.

'Call me what you like. I ought to warn you, Jack isn't going to like this, you busting in here this way. He can be awful mean when he likes.'

'I'll bet.' It was on the tip of my tongue to mention what had happened to Bosun Briggs, but something held me back. 'Look Sally, I'm in a position to make you an offer.'

That seemed to arouse her interest. Her eyes brightened.

'Yeah? What kind of offer?'

'If everything works out right, I can keep you out of this. It's not the first time an older man blew his stack over a girl, and I can see where a man could do that, if you were the girl. The point is, he stole the money, not you. You're in the clear, if I tell it that way. All I want is to know where I can find Joseph P. McEvoy, along with all that lovely money he stole.'

'How much was it altogether?' she demanded.

'Thirty-eight thousand. Didn't you know that?' I asked suspiciously.

'Never mind. Keep talking about this deal.'

'Very well. As I say, I want McEvoy, I want the money. You don't have to figure in this at all. Not your fault if the man went off his chump. On the other hand—'

'What other hand?'

I shrugged.

'Well, if you don't cooperate, there won't be any trouble slapping any number of charges on you. Incitement for one. Conspiracy. Accomplice after the fact. There could be others, too, but I don't want to dwell on all that stuff. You're going to tell me, aren't you?'

She chewed at her lower lip, in the effort of concentration.

'You really mean all this, huh? About McEvoy and so forth?'

'I really do.'

The blue eyes narrowed.

'Suppose I tell you I never heard of this McEvoy?'

'Aw, come on honey. This is kids' stuff. I mean, you have an employment record with the O'Hagan company. All that can be proved in five minutes flat. You oughtn't to waste my time with that nonsense. The point is, do you cooperate or not?'

'I'm thinking.'

She wore a dark blue halter-neck top, leaving her bronzed arms free. As she put a hand up to her chin, muscles rippled into life under the smooth flesh. The photograph was no fake.

'How much time can you give me?' she asked suddenly.

'Why do you need time? Not thinking of

leaving our fair city, I trust? I wouldn't like that, and it would mean cops automatically.'

The blonde head wagged sideways.

'No, I want to think about it. Talk to a lawyer friend. Listen, you're sure there's as much as you say? Thirty-eight thousand?'

'The exact sum,' I assured her.

'Seems to me, if you got it all back, and I was responsible, I ought to come in for some kind of reward.'

It was a promising development. As soon as people start seeing those dollar signs, the end of the road is usually in sight.

'What kind were you thinking of?' I questioned. 'Couple of hundred?'

Neither the expression on her face, nor the one from her lips, was especially ladylike. Then she said—'Couple of thousand, more likely.'

I shook my head.

'That's out. I could try for maybe five hundred. No more.'

'Cheapie.'

All the women in this caper seemed to have that impression of me.

'Well, what do you say?'

'Give me till tomorrow. Want to talk to a man.'

I hesitated. If it really was going to be possible to get back all the money that easily, one more day wouldn't hurt. On the other hand, there was already one murder in the background, if the two were connected, and I thought they were.

'This man you want to talk to, it wouldn't be Jack Durrant, would it?'

Her laugh was short, and contemptuous.

'You have to be kidding. If I let that man know there was any money in this picture, I wouldn't get my hands on a single cent of it. He can be bad news if he smells money.'

'Then you won't be telling him I was here?' I prompted.

'You think I'm crazy? No way.'

I wondered if this girl really was playing a lone hand. Did Durrant know about McEvoy, for instance? Or the other way around. Did the one-time chief cashier know that his girl was playing house with Durrant? In either case, it seemed to me she was fooling around with dynamite. Strictly speaking, it was no skin off my nose, but I felt I couldn't just leave her exposed without some kind of warning.

'Did you hear what happened to Briggs?' I asked suddenly.

If I'd been hoping to catch her off guard, I was disappointed. She only looked blank.

'Briggs? Who's Briggs?'

'Calls himself Bosun,' I added, in case it helped.

'Bosun,' she repeated, 'a sailor? I don't know any sailors. Anyway, you said something happened to him. What was it?'

'He was murdered. Just a few hours ago,' I

95

stated flatly.

She heaved her shoulders.

'Should I feel bad about it? What has that to do with me?'

I had the feeling she was telling the truth, but I've been wrong before.

'He fits in somewhere. I don't know where, but I'll get to it. Anyway, he's dead. I wondered if you might have killed him.'

Her eyes flashed.

'That's it,' she decided. 'Out. Just get out. I'm beginning to think you're some kind of crazy man. Are you going quietly?'

I didn't care at all for the way she was starting to crouch, especially when I thought about the photograph.

'Take it easy,' I cautioned, edging towards the door. 'I'm going. It was only a thought.'

'A crazy thought. The door is behind you.'

'Yes, I'm going. I'll be back tomorrow about the other matter.'

That seemed to relax her a little. Whether I was crazy or not, she still had to deal with me over the McEvoy affair. Me, or the law.

'Leave your crazy ideas home next time.'

I made it out to the hall without any throws.

\*　　\*　　\*

One of the popular attractions of our Paradise by the Pacific (Welcome to Monkton City—a publication by the City Tourist Office—page

96

17) is the genuine London reproduction Olde England Chop House.

Well, that's what it says on Page 17, and it isn't for the likes of me to set up in opposition to the City Tourist Office. When the idea was first touted around, one of our public-spirited councilmen thought the place ought to be located close to the beach. It just so chanced that he had an undeveloped site which would be ideal for the purpose, and he and the City Valuer could get to work on the financial details without delay. Some spoilsport pointed out that the place was supposed to look like a piece of London, England, and that city fell somewhat short in its sandy beach facilities. It was finally decided that the place for the new popular attraction was the business section, and that's where it wound up.

Personally, I was never in Olde England in its chophouse days, which I gather reached a peak around the mid-nineteenth century. Just the same, I have a few reservations about our genuine London reproduction. Probably, I get prejudiced by the six-feet photograph of Samuel Pepys which dominates the lobby, with the Great Fire of London raging in the background. I would have thought the camera work a little expert for his time, and in any case the guy is wearing a wrist watch. The serving wenches now are another matter entirely. Buxom lasses all, and under strict instruction from the management not to conceal the fact. Cover the whole thing in red velvet, with a lot of gold ironwork scattered around, and you begin to get some sense of atmosphere. Scatter a supply of plain deal-topped tables, and fill the air with the aroma of roasting meat and spiced ale. And pewter. Don't overlook the pewter dishes and drinking mugs, because these are the final ingredients. You put a helping of lamb chops on a pewter plate, and a ditto mug of steaming ale alongside, and the customer will gladly pay three times the price he would expect in any other surroundings.

In my city, most of the legitimate business, and most of the other kind, is conducted in a very different establishment called the Trail's End. But if you're in the eat-and-drink line, or the hotel line, and you want to talk about the business behind the business, then you high-tail down to the Olde England Chop House, and seek out Tom Lennard. Back in the great days of Volstead, when the rum was coming up from Panama by sea, and tequila by road from Mexico, there were a number of enterprising men who saw it as no more than a public duty to satisfy the raging thirst which prevailed all down our coastline. Profits were huge, and life expectancy short, so there was even more money to be shared among fewer people. As time went along, the survivors began to diversify their interests, following a classic business principle. The areas they spread money into, at first, were the obvious ones, related to their staple trade, the outlets. With the repeal of prohibition a lot of rum-runners and their ilk found themselves on the unemployed list. But there were others, the smart ones, who were already deep into legitimate enterprises, and they went from strength to strength. First their sons, and lately even the odd grandson, found themselves born into positions of genuine authority. Tom Lennard was not quite one of these. He was a nephew by marriage of Mike 'Two Fingers' Lennard, and as such, entitled to a small share of the big financial cake. But Tom had more of his uncle in him than people gave him credit for, and before long he was moving into the labor area, always good pickings. Old Two Fingers would have been proud of the way the boy struck out on his own, using the same methods that had founded the family fortunes all those years ago.

People will tell you that if you want a licence to operate, a loan to get you started, you must first approach Tom Lennard. They will say that if you want to hire staff, arrange liquor supplies, issue a laundry contract, your first stop is Lennard. They might even go so far as to hint that if you don't do things right, then you will never get your business started, and if you forget who your friends are after you get started, then business becomes very bad quite suddenly.

That's what people will tell you, but then, people will tell you anything. All I know is, Tom Lennard certainly has his finger on the pulse, and he would be the man to know things I wanted to know. He doesn't bother much with his office, a splendid six-roomed suite on Fourth. That's a place for letter-writing, formal conduct of all kinds, and he has plenty of people to deal with all that stuff. His real business is handled in a private dining-room, upstairs in the Chop House. There he holds court every day from noon until three, and there was where I headed.

There is a curved stairway, sweeping up from the street level, and I had one foot on the bottom tread when a pleasant voice said—

'Good afternoon, sir. Could I help you at all?'

He was a smiling man about twenty-five years old, with an open, frank face beneath dark curly hair. I'd never seen him before, but I knew the stamp. Good-looking, well set-up, intelligent, and immaculately dressed. Anywhere else, he would have been the junior partner, the son of the owner, the latest college whizz kid. But at the foot of the stairway leading up to Tom Lennard, he was none of those things. He was the new man, the late twentieth century hood, and he made my stomach crawl.

But I hadn't come there to fight, I reminded me.

'Like a word with Tom Lennard.'

His eyes may have narrowed a fraction.

'Is Mr.,' heavy on the 'Mr.', 'Lennard expecting you?'

'I doubt it. Name is Preston, Mark Preston.'

'What is the nature of your business, Mr. Preston?'

There was annoyance now, and my rising hackles told me there was about to be a ruckus in the lobby of the Olde England Chop House. I told my hackles to mind their manners.

'I doubt whether Tom would want me to discuss his business with the help,' I replied coldly. 'Just tell him I'm here.'

He was better at the control bit than I was. His smile was very thin and icy, but it was a smile.

'If you'll just wait a moment.'

From a small pedestal he picked up a gold-colored old-style telephone, the very kind old Two Fingers would have used to warn his shippers that the coastguard were very active tonight. He mumbled something, keeping his head turned away from me. Then he nodded, as though the guy at the other end could see him, and hung up.

'Are you Mr. Preston the investigator?' he wanted to know.

'The very same,' I confirmed.

'You are to go up, Mr. Preston. Someone will meet you upstairs.'

I went up the gold pile. At the top, heavy

drape curtains covered the landing both sides. Uncertain which way to turn, I looked down. My inquisitor was watching, and he pointed to the right. As I put up a hand to part the curtains, they were lifted aside, and I was looking at a second man, a replica of the one downstairs. Maybe they were brothers.

'You'll be Mr. Preston,' he said knowledgeably.

'I will. And who will you be?'

'I'm Mr. Lennard's nerve specialist,' he assured me solemnly. 'Mr. Lennard gets very nervous around some visitors.'

'Oh really? What kind would that be?'

His smile was even thinner than his brother's.

'The kind that carry weapons, and have been known to shoot them off. That would be your kind, wouldn't it, Mr. Preston?'

I shook my head.

'Not around chop-houses,' I denied. 'This is rapier country.'

'Just the same, you won't mind if I take a little look?'

He patted around here and there, like a man who knew where to pat around. Then his smile widened.

'We just have to be sure, you understand.'

'No offense,' I returned, gravely.

Signalling me to wait, he knocked on a heavy door, and listened to the bellowed response from inside. Then he turned the handle and pushed it open, standing aside for me to enter.

It was a large room, dominated by a huge polished table which ran almost from end to end. Ranged along both sides were heavy upright leather chairs, empty. Facing the door, and that included me, a man sat alone, surrounded by gleaming silver dishes around which lingered savory smells. He was busy trimming the end of a six-inch cigar, and he looked over the top of it to inspect the visitor.

'Come in, come in,' he invited. 'Take a chair. This one.'

He waved me to the place on his left. I walked along the back of the row, and pulled out the indicated chair. Tom Lennard didn't get up, and he didn't offer to shake hands. During my progress down the room, I had a chance to get a good look at him. Seated there, he looked taller than he was, which I knew to be around five feet nine. He had broad shoulders, and thick heavy arms. The thick hands working on the cigar were covered with black wiry hair, and had done a lot heavier work in their time. He hadn't much in the way of neck, the swarthy jowled face sinking almost at once into the shoulders. The eyes were black and sharp, beneath bristling blue-black eyebrows. In earlier days, somebody hadn't cared for the shape of his nose, so they broke it for him, and the result was to give his whole face a sinister twist, even in repose.

He'd been looking at me, too. Now, he

gestured towards the table.

'The British,' he announced solemnly, 'they knew how to eat, them days.'

I inspected the dishes, to see what he'd been eating. One of those scientific Victorian detectives would have worked it out in seconds. To me, all that was on view was some cooling gravy, and a chunk of dismembered fat.

Nodding as though I had the whole picture, I replied—

'I guess that's right.'

'None of your fast food junk for them,' he went on. 'Steaks and pies and good roast beef. I tell you, they just sat around places like this, shovelling away the grub. Then they went out and stole half the world. They couldn't have done that on take-away pizzas, am I right?'

'No argument about it,' I said easily, wondering where all this was leading us.

'Damned right there isn't,' he agreed, as if I'd said something intelligent. 'Where they went, the grub went right along. Even today, in India, you can get a steak and kidney pudding in places where it's a hundred in the shade. Did you know that?'

I tried to look apologetic.

'Well no; I must admit—'

'It was in the Digest,' he interrupted accusingly. 'Whole article about it in there. You missed it, huh?'

A ridiculous idea had thrust its way into my head. Lennard was a new empire-builder, and this was a recruitment drive. Any minute now, I was going to be signing up for the First Lennard Light Horse, and be measured for my sabre or whatever.

'I don't read much these days,' I confessed.

He'd finished fooling around with the weed now, and produced a lighter which gleamed with the dull assurance of solid gold.

'You're a friend of Ben Krantz, they tell me,' he ejaculated, from a cloud of rich blue smoke.

'We go back a long time,' I confirmed.

'What I hear, what I hear,' he said repetitiously. 'Matter of fact, that's how you got in here. How is Ben these days?'

'Pretty fair,' I contributed cautiously. 'That stomach of his doesn't seem to improve much.'

Lennard waved this away with impatience.

'Pah,' he snorted. 'The man don't eat right. What does he expect? I told him once, I told him twenty times. Ben, I told him, you ain't never gonna get no better while you keep noshing those pigs' knuckles. He can be very stubborn, that Ben.'

Since I'd passed on exactly the same advice more than once, I could do nothing but agree. And with embellishments.

'Told him the same myself. He ought to be trying the devilled lamb chops, that's what I've said.'

Lennard narrowed his eyes suspiciously, then his cheeks swelled out, and he produced an explosive laugh.

'You and me could get along,' he chuckled. 'It all depends on what it is you want. What is it?'

This was the point of sale. Everything else was just window-dressing, for the casual shoppers.

'I'm trying to find a man,' I explained. 'He took off with a lot of money that didn't belong to him. He's a bonded employee, and that makes it police business, insurance business, everybody's business.'

His features remained impassive.

'What makes it your business?' he enquired, almost casually.

'Ten per cent of the bond. If I find him, I collect twenty-five hundred dollars.'

I like to hang out those dollar signs at an early stage. It gives people confidence in my motives.

'H'm. I don't recollect hearing about this guy. Is it an old case, or a very new case, maybe?'

I shook my head.

'The local papers wouldn't have bothered. This man is from San Francisco.'

'Ah.' He exhaled smoke, nodding. 'That's why I don't know. Well, he's a long way from those golden gates. What makes you think he's around here?'

'There's a dame.'

I left it at that. In certain circles, it is always

sufficient explanation in itself, to mention that a lady is involved.

Lennard removed the cigar from his mouth, and held it in front of him.

'I'm still listening.'

'The girl is somehow involved with the Bear-Bear Club. It's a new place, which you know better than I do. New place means new people, new money.'

'And you figure your bond jumper could be putting up the dough? Is that why you're here?'

'It's a possibility.'

He leaned back, resting his arms on the burnished brown leather of the chair.

'Look, people come to me in the way of business. I don't ask where the money comes from. No skin off my nose, just so it's there. How long do you think I'd stay open if I went around poking my nose into other people's affairs?'

But I'd been expecting a stall of that kind, and had my story all pat.

'Normally yes, I agree. And normally I wouldn't come here wasting your time. But this is not quite normal. The police up in San Francisco have a theory that this employee did not skip out of his own accord. They think he may have been kidnapped. And you know what that means. A snatch job is a Federal offense, and that makes it tough all round.'

It was a lucky thing for me that no

policeman from the city across the bay was listening to my fanciful story. It seemed to be having its effect on Lennard, though. The banana fingers drummed on leather while he thought about it.

'Federal, huh? Well, nobody needs those people sniffing around. They don't bring nothing but grief. You think they're looking this way?'

This was the time for my hole card. If it didn't work, I would lose the pot. I shook my head very seriously.

'At the moment, no. This lead is confidential to me. If I can crack the case, there'll be no need for any Feds, no need for anybody else at all. We can keep everything in the family.'

He spotted what he thought was a flaw in that argument.

'Sure. If you crack it. But if you don't? What then?'

'Why then I close the file. Very quietly. Like I just said, nobody else knows about this lead. If it turns out to be a bust, I don't want egg all over my face. You may not think so, but I have some kind of reputation to think about.'

'Yeah.'

He liked it. I'd given him an opportunity to catch me out, as he saw it, and I'd been ready for it. Now, he spoke again.

'So, if I tell you to forget it, that's the end, huh?'

'Well, more or less,' I agreed.

'How's that?'

'I mean, if you say so, that's good enough for me. But I would just feel better if you told me why.'

Freed of any suspicion that his word was being challenged, he became expansive.

'Oh, sure. Sure. Well, I'll tell you. The guy behind the Bear-Bear Club is no bond jumper. He's a small-time entertainer, name of Jack Durrant. I had him checked out before any deal went through. The guy is a hustler, been around for years. If he was holding anybody on a snatch, believe me, I would know. I guess that's it. You'll have to think some more, huh?'

The interview, it seemed, was at an end. I got up to leave.

'Like I said, your word is good enough in this town. Thanks for your time. I won't be doing or saying anything to point the Federals this way.'

Which was nothing but the plain truth.

When I got to the door, he waved. On the way downstairs, I had plenty to think about.


# EIGHT

It was high time I looked in at the office. It was all very well, the way I was cavorting hither and thither, with or without the delectable Abigail, but it wasn't very business-like.

Florence Digby might be no more than a paid retainer in the eyes of the Revenue Department, but to me she was also a hard taskmaster. Florence does not like me to go calling here and there and round and about, without some cause to which she can allocate my valuable time. On a dollars per day basis, that is. It was easy for me to justify all this by pointing out that it was her absence from the desk that allowed the devastating O'Hagan to slip through the net in the first place. That had been over twenty-four hours earlier, and I hadn't been near the office since.

So I was all girded up for a fairly brisk interview with La Digby when I sidled into the office in mid-afternoon. Despite the heat outside, Florence was as cool and immaculate as ever, in a severe tailored blouse that looked as if it had just been unwrapped.

'Oh, afternoon Florence,' I mumbled. 'Guess things kind of caught up with me—'

To my astonishment, she smiled.

'Yes. I understand you've been very busy, Mr. Preston. Miss O'Hagan has explained the McEvoy case, and I have opened a new file.'

I blinked foolishly.

'Miss O'Hagan?' I repeated.

'Yes. She came in about an hour ago. What a delightful young woman. So efficient, so business-like. It's a pity not all of our clients could be described in the same terms.'

'Right,' I agreed heartily. 'Well, how would

it be if you came into my office for a few minutes, and we can both kind of catch up?'

Florence rose at once, and followed me through. What I really wanted was to find out what kind of yarn the appalling Abigail had been pitching. In the event, it wasn't too bad. The main bones of the enquiry were just as Florence had them.

'And, simply as a matter of completeness—' she continued—

—that meant out of sheer idle curiosity, I amended—

'—I checked the background of the O'Hagan Machine Company. Mr. O'Hagan has a Gold Band credit rating in every area.'

Which made Mr. O'Hagan very much O.K. with a certain confidential secretary.

'Good for him,' I replied, trying not to sound too sour. One of these days I'm going to put out an enquiry on myself, but I'm never absolutely certain I want to hear the answer. Somehow I don't see that Gold Band shining through. Except with the bookmakers, of course.

'Did Miss O'Hagan say where she was going when she left here?' I asked.

Florence looked smug.

'She wanted to do some shopping. I was able to advise her about which of our stores were worthy of a visit.'

I'll bet, I reacted. Still, mustn't get grouchy. Abigail had got me off the hook with the

Digby, which was one good thing. She had also gone off shopping, which would keep her out of my hair for the next few hours. And that was another good thing. Out loud I said—

'That was nice of you. Being a stranger in town, she would appreciate that. How're things, generally? Any new stuff coming through?'

Florence left the acceptable subject of Abigail H. O'Hagan with evident reluctance, and looked at her notebook.

'There was a telephone call this morning, at eleven forty. A woman'—not a lady, I noticed—'calling herself Lolita Montez wished to speak with you. When I told her you were not in the office, she seemed quite put out.'

Frosty eyes inspected me. We were through with O'Hagan now, and back in the more dubious Montez territory, where Florence clearly thought I more properly belonged.

'Montez?' I repeated, trying to recall.

'Yes. I must say Mr. Preston, the accent was not particularly Spanish. To be more specific, there was no trace of an accent whatever.'

Montez. I had it now. That was the stage name used by Briggs' sister Betty. The girl I'd met backstage at the Bear-Bear Club, and who had subsequently set the dogs after me.

'What did she want?' I asked.

'She would not confide in me,' was the lofty reply. 'I rather gathered the impression it was a personal matter.'

And when the Digby gathers that impression, particularly with somebody like the un-Spanish Lolita, my credit rating goes out of the window. Well, she could think what she liked.

'Did she leave a number?'

The finely drawn eyebrows lifted two millimetres.

'Yes, I have it here. I thought possibly—'

'—I would already know it,' I finished tartly. 'Well, I don't. See if you can raise her for me, please.'

It was a comfort to see her feeling slightly puzzled as she went out. I was wondering what Lolita would want with me. What was it Briggs had called her? Betty. That was it. Betty Briggs. A far cry from Lolita Montez, by any stretch of the imagination. Maybe this was going to be a blackmail attempt. She had put her brother in touch with me, and a few hours later, he got himself killed. That would be enough to set a policeman thinking bad thoughts. There was unlikely to be any way she could know that the lawmen had already caught up with me from quite different sources. Then again, it may not be that at all. She may have some new information to peddle, and I was certainly in the market for it.

The phone blatted.

'Preston,' I announced.

'I'm sorry Mr. Preston, I'm getting no reply from that number,' came Florence's voice.

'O.K. thanks. We'll try again later.'

It would have to be much later, I reminded myself. At that moment, I was about to go out. I wanted to know more about Jack Durrant's background and activities. The one person I'd met so far who should be able to help me was the little agent with the impossible name of Antonio Schwarz.

Conquest Street hadn't improved any since the previous day. It was just as torn and tattered, just as heavy with the smell of a thousand stale dishes and cheap booze. I locked the car with great care, under the inspection of a sprawling brute of a man who was making desultory cleaning motions at the windows of the topless disco. He would have to be new, I decided. On Conquest, only new people make even a pretense of cleaning windows.

Seven o nine was where I'd left it. About the only thing on Conquest that can't be stolen is the structure. I made noise on the stairway again, and went into Schwarz' magic parlor, the ante room to the glittering world of show business. The chief magician had his scuffed shoes up on the desk, and was picking at his nails when I arrived. His sad face brightened a little at my entrance. Well, not strictly at my entrance, but in the spot over my shoulder where he hoped Abigail was going to appear.

'Hi, Antonio,' I greeted.

'No Sugar Plum today?' he queried.

'She's trying out for some floor-show this afternoon,' I hedged. 'Today, all you get is me.'

He dismissed me with one wave.

'You, I don't need. I got all the brothers I can handle.'

I nodded cheerfully, and sat down in the one vacant chair, which squeaked in protest, but stopped short of actual collapse.

'Nobody told you to get comfortable,' he said nastily.

'Now, now, Antonio,' I reproved, 'that's no way to speak to people. Let's understand one another. I'm one of the brothers you can't handle, so don't waste everybody's time trying.'

He scowled, and swung his feet to the floor.

'I got nothing to talk to you about.'

'We can't be sure of that until we try,' I corrected cheerfully. 'Now, I'm going to ask one or two questions, and you're going to give me one or two answers. Are you catching the idea?'

'Oh, I see.'

Schwarz nodded, as though digesting this new information. Then he leaned forward casually, opened a drawer, and took out a Colt six-chambered revolver, which he pointed in my general direction.

'I don't like you,' he explained. 'Go away.'

I've looked at a lot of guns. They don't interest me half as much as the faces behind them. Schwarz' face was strained and sweating.

The eyes were anxious, darting all over me, as if looking for suitable vacant lots for lead to be planted in.

'Take it easy, Antonio,' I advised. 'Those things have the damndest habit of going off and hurting people. Then where would you be?'

His hand was quite steady.

'I would be a business man who got attacked by some stranger twice his size. I would be a guy who had to defend himself the best he could.'

I smiled, with all the conviction a scared man can muster.

'You think they'll accept that?' I queried. 'You think they'll stand for you wasting a police officer that way?'

'Huh?'

His jaw dropped slightly, and the gun wavered. I waited.

'That's on the level? You're some kind of copper?'

My smile was gaining in confidence all the time.

'I am a Deputy Sheriff of Huache County, and I have identification right in my pocket, if you'll let me take it out.'

Now he passed a hand over his chin, to indicate thought.

'Huache County is two hundred miles from here,' he objected. 'You don't have no jurisdiction in this city.'

'That's true, about jurisdiction,' I agreed. 'But a copper is always a copper, wherever he goes. These local boys won't take it kindly, you rubbing out a visiting officer.'

'Open the coat,' he instructed, peremptorily. I did so.

'Which side is this famous identification?' I pointed inside with a forefinger.

'Take it out, real slow, and show me.'

I was very careful with the leather. Then I rifled through until I found what I was looking for. Years before, I'd been over in Huache on an insurance gig. The sheriff and I hit it off on sight, and we cleaned up a problem in a matter of hours. I split the reward money with him, and we had a royal session which lasted most of the night. To conclude the festivities, I was appointed an honorary deputy sheriff of the county. This high office carries about the same weight as a Junior Dick Tracy badge, but it looks official enough, and can come in handy under certain circumstances. Like now. I tossed the printed document over and Schwarz looked at it doubtfully.

'If you're a cop, why didn't you say so yesterday? And where does Sugar Plum fit in? Don't tell me she's the fire chief's daughter?'

'No, no,' I laughed, noting the lowered angle of the gun barrel. 'She's the real thing, just like she says. Can't blame her for what her brother does, huh?'

He rested the Colt on the table top, where

he could reach it, and I couldn't.

'All right, so I don't want cop trouble,' he assented unhappily. 'What is it you want, that I'm not going to give you?'

It was only a stand-off. He wasn't ready to capitulate. Not yet.

'To start with, you could tell me why you started waving that thing about? I wasn't threatening you. Somebody else must have told you I was trouble. Who was it?'

'I know what I know,' he said stubbornly. 'Next question?'

I stared at him without love.

'Do you know what this is all about, Antonio? Did your good friend mention murder?'

He didn't care for the word at all.

'Murder?'

'Murder. Murder One. And, if you don't understand the expression, it means murder in the first degree. That's the worst there is, Antonio, and you're shaping up to be an accomplice.'

Now, some confidence returned to the screwed-up features. He sneered.

'Accomplice? Me? You're crazy. I don't know nothing about no murder, I never had nothing to do with no murder. You're crazy, is what. A business man, that's me. Go peddle your papers.'

I sighed at that, making a show of heavy patience.

'Schwarz, believe me, I'm trying to help you, but you have to kick back. Personally, I doubt whether you're mixed up in this—'

'—well, there you are, you see—'

'—don't interrupt me. The point is, the boys downtown won't care what I think. What they care is what they think. When they find out you are concealing evidence material to the solution of a case of murder, they will slap an accessory charge on you, just for openers.'

Antonio Schwarz was paying very careful attention.

'Concealing what evidence?' he queried, but without great conviction. 'Like I told you, I don't know nothing about no murder. Dammit, I don't even know who got scragged.'

I pulled out my Old Favorites, and lit one slowly. His hand rested lightly on the Colt while my own was busy in the pocket area.

'Let's try again,' I suggested. 'Let's talk about Jack Durrant.'

At the mention of the name, his fingers flexed slightly.

'What about him?'

'You're his agent. You ought to know where he's been working lately.'

'You already know that,' he objected. 'He's out at this new place.'

'No, no, I mean before that. Somebody said he was doing a stint up in San Francisco.'

'Oh, that.' He looked relieved. Evidently he could see no harm in talking about the past.

119

'Sure, he was up there for—let's see—ten weeks or so. He was working a double up there, with some dame. It's history. What about it?'

The mention of a woman was intriguing.

'Who was the woman,' I asked, 'does she have a name?'

'Oh sure,' he shrugged. 'I imagine she does. I never seen her. I just pay Jack his money. What he pays the help is his business.'

I wondered if he was concealing something.

'Are you trying to tell me that some girl can work through this agency, and you don't even know who she is?' I demanded nastily.

There was nothing forced about his smile now.

'You have to be kidding. In this business, the dames come along with the ashtrays and the tablecloths. When you're through with one, you throw her away, and get another one. Names, he wants. Listen, half of these entertaining ladies couldn't remember their own names on a bet.' He swivelled round in his chair, and jabbed a finger towards the beauty chorus on the wall. 'You see that bunch up there? I don't know where half of them are, as of this minute. I don't even know for sure what names they're using.'

He stuck his wise little head at an angle, to see whether I was catching the drift. I was, and it wasn't promising. But the introduction of the photographs had put an idea in my head.

'Take your point,' I conceded. 'But this act of Durrant's, would you have a picture of that?'

Schwarz shrugged.

'I guess so. Be around here someplace. The filing ain't what it ought to be.'

By way of demonstration, he pulled a large cardboard box from a shelf. It was full of photographs of all shapes and sizes, jumbled up every which way. He poked around for a while, pulling out one every now and then, for inspection. Sometimes he would wince, or give a chuckle, at whatever kind of recollection the picture provoked. Finally, he pulled out a shot of a man and a woman, smiling and half-bowing to an unseen audience. The audience was now me, and I wasted no time on Durrant's artificial grin. It was the girl I wanted to see, and the girl was Sally Dewes. Stage make-up or no, there was no mistaking the girl I'd spoken with just a few hours before. Above the heads of the performers was a sign reading 'Club Hotfoot Presents'.

'Thought you said you didn't know Sally Dewes?' I asked.

'That's what I said, and that's what I meant,' countered Schwarz, not remotely concerned. 'Listen, that Durrant eats dames the way some. guys eat candy.'

I frowned again at the photograph.

'According to this, she works with him in the act.'

'Not any more. He's strictly single-o now. Let me see that.' He took the picture back, frowning. 'Yeah. That's right. This is the joint Durrant was working in San Francisco. She must have been some local girl. One thing you gotta say for that city. There's no shortage of dames.'

But I still had an objection.

'This girl had a regular job,' I insisted. 'I even know the name of the company she worked for.'

If I'd expected to fase him, I was to be disappointed.

'So what?' he countered. 'Lots of people have regular jobs. They finish at what time? Five, five thirty? Then they put on the glad rags, and make like actors. Especially the dames. It's a chance to see the bright lights, earn a few bucks, where's the harm?'

That would make sense. If Sally Dewes was working with Durrant in the evenings, she could have told him about her daytime job. She could have told him about the cashier, McEvoy, making a play for her. It wasn't hard to imagine Durrant putting all that information together, and coming up with a touch of larceny. I was beginning to like it.

'Could I keep the picture?'

Schwarz sighed.

'Cost you a buck. I can't afford to hand out this stuff for nothing.'

I took out a dollar bill, and handed it over.

'I can see where you're really going to make it big in this business. You have a certain breadth of vision.'

'These are hard times,' he assured me. 'And a buck is a buck.'

It seemed to me I wasn't going to learn much more about Jack Durrant, on this visit. Already, I was doing fine. But there was still one other question to be asked. 'Tell me, does Lolita Montez work through you?'

'The juggler? What about her?'

'Nothing, really. I caught her act the other night. Pretty good. If you have a picture of her, I have another dollar.'

He didn't hesitate this time, diving at once into his cardboard box.

'That one I got. She's new in town. Been working over in Vegas these past few months, but the action got a little rough.'

'Oh? What made her choose our fair city to run to?'

He scratched at his cheek, thinking.

'Think she said something about having some family here. I didn't pay no attention, not really. These dames'll tell you anything.'

'A brother, maybe? Did she say she had a brother here?'

'Could be,' he admitted. 'Like I said, I wasn't listening. Ah, there you go.'

He pulled out a shiny photograph of the girl I'd spoken with when I was looking for Jack Durrant. I took it from him. Lolita looked even better when she was posing for posterity.

'What's with her and Durrant?' I queried. 'A little something going there?'

Antonio grinned.

'She's a dame, ain't she? He's got to make a pitch. With him, it's like what you might call a nervous reaction.'

We grinned, like a couple of nervous reactors.

'Well thanks, Antonio. All this is a big help.'

'What about the law?' he asked, nervously. 'All this murder chat, that was some kind of gag, huh?'

I shook my head with great seriousness.

'No gag, believe me. I'm going to give you a piece of advice. I know you won't tell me who it was told you I was bad news. Watch your step with that one. A person who's already committed murder won't think twice about a second one, if it'll cover tracks. You want to tell me who it was?'

'Nobody told me,' he denied. 'It was just a feeling I had.'

I heaved my shoulders.

'Well, you know your own business. But I'd feel bad if something terrible was to happen to you. Do me a favor. Carry that piece around with you for the next day or two.'

He looked horrified.

'Me? Carry a gun? Listen, you think I'm Al Capone or somebody?'

'No, I don't, Antonio. I'm just talking for

your own good.'

I left him sitting there, a worried frown on the wizened features.

On the way out, I was feeling one step ahead, for a change. Things were beginning to break at last. On top of that, I now had the advantage over a certain Abigail H. O'Hagan, because I knew things she didn't know.

When I reached the car, I was actually whistling.

You'd think a man would learn.

# NINE

By the time I got back in the center of town, it was too late to go back to the office. Florence Digby would have locked up and gone, and there was nothing there I needed right then. Instead, I headed for Parkside, and was enjoying turning over in my mind the way I was going to play it with Abigail. She'd had a good run for her money, and it had been amusing to let her score her little points in unimportant areas. Now that the real work was beginning, and that old pay dirt was beginning to glitter among the dross, it was time for the professional to show his hand. Time to let my shining amateur friend see what really happens in a case of this kind, to let her see the great gumshoe at work.

125

I called out her name as I let myself in. There was no response. I looked in the kitchen and the bedroom. No Abigail. There were also no parcels on view, as I would have expected when a woman has been shopping. The time was a little after six thirty, and I poured myself a weak drink, wondering where the whizz-girl could be hiding. The trouble with that girl was, she was so unpredictable. She'd go running off at some tangent, if the fancy took her. Considering that there was already one dead man in the picture, I found my imagination readily conjuring up all kinds of trouble she could be causing. Mainly to herself. It's fair to say I was getting myself worked up about her safety when, at a few minutes before seven, a key turned in the lock.

'Hi,' she greeted, all smiles, 'have you been back very long?'

Just like that. No 'I'm sorry to have ducked out on you that way'. No 'I hope you weren't worried about me'. Nothing of the kind. Just a breezy greeting, and a cloud of perfumed freshness as she crossed the room, dumping parcels—oh yes, we had parcels now—and sitting down with an inelegant snort.

'Aren't you going to ask me where I've been?' she teased.

I tried not to sound peevish.

'Damned right I am. What do you mean, going off that way? It may just have slipped your memory, but this is a case of murder. A man has been killed, O'Hagan, and that means the rules have been changed.'

'Rules?'

'Rules,' I repeated positively. 'I didn't object to your flouncing around my territory, doing your campus kid imitation, while we were just looking for some harmless chump. Things are different now. Somewhere out there is a man with a gun. He kills people, and you are not going to be one of them. Not while I can stop it. From now on, you will stay here and darn socks, unless I say otherwise.'

I stopped then. I wasn't really finished, but I needed to breathe. Abigail regarded me frostily.

'First thing I'll do is to get your M.C.P. armband washed and pressed,' she replied.

Knowing I was going to regret having asked, I said—

'M.C.P.? What is that?'

'Male chauvinist pig,' she informed me, with relish. 'You are the president of the local chapter, aren't you? Where do you get off with this sock routine? Darn your own. And another thing, who says the person with a gun is a man? That's typical of people like you. You think a woman can't pull a trigger? Last I heard of it, a four-year-old-child could do it.'

'That is correct,' I snapped. 'There's a list of all the homicidal four-year-olds being circulated right now. I had to use a lot of influence to keep your name off it.'

We both breathed heavily, and sat staring dislike across the room. For my part, I didn't know why I should bother with her. Headstrong, arrogant, impulsive. Totally unreliable as to what she might be expected to do in a given situation. She could get her head blown off out there, the way she barged around, planting her great feet in any wet cement that got in the way. Why should I care? There was no valid reason why it should bother me if this unpredictable bombshell should get wasted. I mean, look at the way she reacted at that moment. No contrition. No sign of any awareness of having broken any of the rules. All I was getting out of this exchange was glared defiance.

Well, somebody was going to have to speak first, and it wasn't my turn.

'Is that it?' she demanded.

'That's about it.'

'Can I take it you're through now, with this gauleiter act? Or do I hear the jackboots stamping up the stairs?'

'Don't be childish,' I snapped. 'All that's happening here is, you're being told to behave yourself. This murder puts the case out of your league. You will do only what I consider to be safe.'

'We'll see about that,' she retorted darkly. 'Anyway, I shall be too busy with my new job.'

Job? What had she done now?

'What do you mean, job?'

'I mean what I say. My new employment will keep me occupied, while you're out mixing with your killer friends.'

She wasn't going to elaborate on that, unless I pressed. Knowing that I was not going to like the answer, I asked—

'All right. Tell me what you're up to now.'

My opponent bridled, like some Southern belle in one of those war-between-the-states movies.

'Why suh, Ah cain't imagine what you-all are suggesting. Up to? Fie on you, suh. Ah am not up to anything. Ah have simply adopted a useful occupation.'

'Bette Davis was better at it,' I told her unkindly. 'What do you call a useful occupation?'

The crack about Miss Davis spared me any further use of the accent.

'I'm the new featured attraction at a leading night spot,' she advised me coolly. 'If they like me tonight, I get my name up outside, and a guaranteed three weeks.'

It was difficult to keep the dismay out of my voice.

'Would I perhaps know this fun-palace?'

Abigail frowned doubtfully.

'I don't know whether you would. We normally aim for a better class of person. It's called the Bear-Bear Club.'

As had been inevitable from the start. I held up my hands in submission.

'All right. Once more, from the top, and play it slowly.'

She nodded brightly, having regained the upper hand.

'Well, I got to thinking, you see. This man Durrant is one key figure in all this. He obviously knows more than he's telling us—no, that's not quite right.'

'Yes it is,' I contradicted.

'No,' she demurred. 'I should have said he knows more than he's telling you. That's not the same thing. I haven't tried yet, remember?'

'You think he'll tell you everything, just because you have a pretty face?'

The said face beamed with delight.

'Oh, do you think so? Would you care to discuss that a little further? I mean, what about the rest of me?'

I snorted with frustration.

'For Pete's sake, stick to the point. Durrant wouldn't talk to me. What makes you think he'll talk to you?'

'Oh,' she waved a dismissive hand, 'I don't think he will for a minute. Not knowingly, that is. I mean, if I were to walk in there with all that lawyer O'Hagan stuff, he'd probably clam up. But a girl from the floorshow, she's another proposition entirely. I won't be asking him any direct questions. I'll just be around him a lot, especially when he's drinking. You told me yourself that he spent a lot of time doing that.'

It had been Lolita Montez who indicated as much to me when we were backstage.

'That's what I hear,' I confirmed. 'But go on telling me about this job.'

'Well, it seemed to me, if I could approach friend Durrant from an entirely different angle, I might have more luck. So I took a ride out there this afternoon, and talked him into letting me dance for him. I drew a lot of applause last night, and I knew he would have heard about it. It seemed to be worth a try. As it turned out, I picked the moment exactly right. The juggler girl, Lolita something—'

'—Montez,' I supplied.

She sneered.

'I might have expected you to know that. You were halfway out of your chair when she was doing her act last night.'

'Are we talking about the same girl?' I asked. 'About five six, one hundred and thirty pounds, face rather like a Greek goddess, with a figure to match? Long sensuous arms, with the most amazing hands? Head of hair like spun gold? I scarcely noticed her at all.'

'That's the one,' she confirmed. 'I'm surprised you remember.'

'It's my detective training,' I told her smugly. 'Anyway, what about her?'

Reluctantly, she got back to the point.

'She called in to say she was sick, and wouldn't be able to do her show tonight. It sounded a bit off-beat to me.'

'Oh, why?'

I was trying to remember whether I'd told Abigail about Lolita being the sister of the deceased Briggs, and couldn't recall having done that.

'So far as I could make out, Jack had sent someone round to her apartment—' ah, it was 'Jack' now—'and she wasn't home. Most sick people stay at home.'

'Unless they've been hospitalised,' I pointed out. She pouted in disbelief.

'If that was the case, she'd have said so, surely?'

'Not necessarily. These show people are very reluctant to admit being sick, as a general rule. John Public isn't interested in their troubles. He pays to see a performance, not a medical certificate.'

'Yes, I can see that. Well, no matter. It's an ill wind, dah-de-dah. One minus Lolita equals one plus Abigail. Or, I should say, Sugarplum La Chatte.'

I didn't have to fake surprise.

'Sugarplum La Chatte?' I echoed, appalled.

'Sure. It's French. Gives the act a touch of class. I come on wearing these feathers you see—'

'Cats don't have feathers,' I pointed out, with cutting logic.

'This is a French cat. What do you know about French cats?' she riposted. 'So I'm wearing these blue and silver feathers—'

'I hope you moult.'

'Why sugar, that is the entiah idea,' she informed me sweetly. 'Jack is very insistent about that. He even gave me a numbered sequence for the moulting process. Now the first one drops off here.'

She pointed to her shoulder.

'You can spare me the sordid details,' I said huffily. 'And what happened to that deal we had this morning? You seemed to understand then how dangerous this is all getting. Now you're sticking your neck right out. Well, if somebody cuts your throat, don't come crying to me about it. You've been told, and that's it.'

Why should I bother about her? She was wilful, obstinate, and now reckless. Well, if she wasn't going to reck, there was no reason why I should. She received this message with wide-eyed scepticism.

'How can a body cry with a cut throat?' she demanded. 'Anyway, you're only jealous, because I'm so much better at this detection business than you are. I'm right in there where the action is. What have you got to show the audience?'

'That's just it,' I countered. 'The trick in this business is never to show your hand. My, my, is that the time? Hadn't you better be pressing your feathers?'

'No hurry. I don't go on till ten thirty.'

'Well, I have to make a call.'

It was time I tried the number Lolita

Montez had left with Florence. I didn't know whether she'd be able to get me any further forward, but at this stage of the game I couldn't afford not to follow through. There was no answer, so I dialled a man I know in the telephone company.

'Hallo Mac, this is Mark Preston. How you been? Good. Yes, me too! Look, Mac, I have a number, but I need an address to go with it.' I read out the number, and he told me to hang on. In no time, he was back with the address, plus the information that Lolita was listed as Elizabeth Briggs. 'I really appreciate this, Mac. Buy you a beer some time.'

He muttered something ungracious about me being a fool with my money, and severed the connection. Abigail had made no bones about her close interest in the call.

'Whose address is that you just got?' she demanded.

'It's the registered office of the Fur and Feather Society,' I said blandly.

'No it isn't. I'm a protected species, and I ought to know. It's somebody we have to go visit, right?'

'Wrong. It's somebody I have to visit. You can stay here and practise your moulting.'

She didn't actually stamp her foot, but that was only because she was sitting down at the time.

'Oh, you.' She did actually toss her head. 'You give me all this talk about looking after

134

me, but if you really meant it, you'd want me where you could see me the whole time. This is your apartment, right? This murderer probably knows you're mixed up in the case, right? So if he comes around here looking for you, and finds me, I could be in real danger, right?'

What is it about some people that makes them think if they use the word 'right' often enough, then it adds truth to whatever it is they're saying?

'You said "right" three times,' I pointed out. 'Three rights don't make a wrong.'

Just the same, she had me worried. There was an element of truth in what she had said, and I wasn't expecting any trouble while paying a call on the delectable Lolita. It was almost as if Abigail suspected what was going on in my mind. Normally, she would have cracked straight back at me, but this time she just sat there, looking smug, and waited.

'All right,' I conceded, with reluctance. 'There's no harm in your tagging along. Just don't interfere, agreed?'

'You got it,' she said brightly. 'Absolutely.'

With her record to date in that direction, I didn't believe a word of it. She waited until we were in the car before asking who we were going to see.

'Sick visit,' I told her. 'Calling on your pal, Lolita Montez.'

'Oh Mark, and you're letting me come with

135

you?' She squeezed my arm affectionately. 'Now I believe you really do care what happens to me. Imagine you, passing up an opportunity to be alone with the lady juggler.'

'It's only because she's sick,' I objected. 'If this lady was fit, you'd have to go and find your own juggler.'

But she didn't let go of my arm. I liked that.

The address I had from Mac was that of a one-roomed apartment block on the wrong side of town. The place wasn't what you'd call run down, not yet, but that was the direction the arrow was pointing.

'Not exactly the Ritz, is it?' observed Abigail, as we got out.

'It's about right, for jugglers and feather artists,' I said snidely.

In the lobby, a man sat reading a newspaper. When we marched in, he said—

'You're not residents, so you have to be visitors. Mind if I ask who you're visiting?'

'Mind if I ask what makes it your business?' I retorted.

But I already knew the answer, even before he held out that silver shield.

'Could we try again?' he asked. 'Who've you come to see?'

'Miss Briggs,' I replied.

'Miss Montez,' contributed Abigail.

I glared at her.

The plain clothes man stood up and looked at each of us in turn. My manly features impressed themselves at once. He took a little longer with my companion.

'Well now, which is it?' he queried.

'It's both,' I admitted. 'Miss Briggs is the lady's real name. She calls herself Montez while she's working. She's in show business.'

'That a fact?' he returned impressively. 'Well, that's very interesting, and my boss is very anxious to talk to you folks. You won't mind just stepping around to headquarters? Shouldn't take too long. Oh, and—er—your names, please?'

A polite flatfoot. There are all kinds, and they come with all attitudes. I've dealt with them all, and believe me, the polite ones are the most dangerous.

'I don't see—' began Abigail, but I shushed her.

'What have we got to lose? You wouldn't want this officer to think we don't cooperate with the police, now would you?'

He had a partner waiting outside in an unmarked car.

'You folks use your own car,' was the instruction. 'Do you know where police headquarters are?'

I told him I did, and he nodded.

'My partner will follow you there. Good of you to cooperate.'

As though we had an alternative.

# TEN

It was a short drive, and soon we were climbing up that rickety stairway leading to the three poky rooms with the grand designation of Homicide Bureau. Our escort must have radioed ahead, because Lieutenant John Rourke was waiting for us when we marched in.

Rourke is a grizzled, wiry Irishman, with thirty years of hard coppering behind him. He carries the title of Captain of Detectives, but the penny-pinching administration kept his actual paid rank as Lieutenant. When he saw me come through the door, he winced. But he brightened up considerably when Abigail appeared. They all do. He even stood up.

'Well, well, if it isn't the great detective. Just dropping around to give a few pointers to the local flatfeet, eh?'

But he wasn't mean today, and that was a good sign.

'Just cooperating one hundred per cent with the law, as always,' I assured him. 'How are you, John?'

'How am I John?' he mimicked. 'I'll tell you how am I. I'm puzzled, that's how am I. Let's all sit down, and talk about it.'

Abigail grabbed the one good chair. I dragged up the other one, the one they normally reserve for suspects they don't like. It's hard, uneven, and shaky. In addition to that, one of the legs has poked its way through the seat half an inch, so that no matter how much a man shifts round, that wood is sticking in him somewhere. Thirty minutes on that chair, and anybody will confess to anything.

'Time you sprung some new furniture,' I grumbled.

Rourke tutted.

'We'd hate to be a burden on the taxpayers. I trust this young lady isn't uncomfortable?'

That brought him one of those smiles of hers, and Rourke isn't so old he can't be reached.

'I'm just fine, thank you, Captain.'

He beamed at her.

'I'll ask you, in a few minutes, what a fine young girl like yourself is doing in such company. You just sit and be comfortable, meantime. Now then, Mr. Preston, this is an odd business, you turning up again. Like to tell me about it?'

I didn't like him being nice. And I didn't like being called 'Mr.'.

'Tell you about what? There's no law against calling on people.'

He nodded, as though I'd said something profound.

'That's very true, is that. But look at it from my point of view. A man calls you on the telephone. You go and talk with him. Next thing we're all surprised to hear, the man is dead. You know nothing about that, naturally—'

'—damn right—' I cut in.

'—yes, but look at this new development. The dead man has a sister, who's turned up missing. And what do we find? We find you calling on the lady. Now that's an odd coincidence, wouldn't you say?'

It was all going to have to come out now. I could stall for a while, but in the end Rourke was going to get the story. I might have to say goodbye to my twelve hundred and fifty dollars, but it wasn't enough money to justify my taking too high an attitude. My real concern was to protect Abigail from a concealment charge.

'I wondered whether Briggs may have told his sister anything about the Prentice robbery. Just an outside chance.'

'Oh?' he nodded, not believing a word of it. 'Odd though, you'll admit. The average street informer doesn't go around handing out his sister's home address to every Tom, Dick and Preston. That's for people in another line of work entirely. Plus, this sister doesn't even use her right name most of the time. Seems she's some kind of entertainer. Works at a place called the Bear-Bear Club. I had an officer out there today, looking for her. Guess what he told me? He told me you were out there last night. One of the waiters recognised you, because you helped send up his brother a year or two back, and a man doesn't forget little favors like that. Now, I don't mind a little coincidence here, a little coincidence there, but when there's too many of 'em, it makes me think bad thoughts. I'm thinking them now. About you. Try talking some more.'

He jabbed a finger at me. Before I could speak, Abigail jumped in.

'Excuse me Captain, but I think I can help you there.'

Reluctantly he pulled his gaze away from me, and turned towards her.

'You, miss? It's Miss O'Hagan, isn't it? A fine Irish name.'

She had the damned effrontery to flutter her eyelashes at him.

'Why thank you. Well now, the reason Mr. Preston was out at that place last night was to help me.'

She stopped there, as if she'd explained something. In Rourke's book, she hadn't got properly started.

'To help you, you say? Help you to do what, miss?'

'I came here to find a missing friend. She has been in show business in the past, and I thought if we went round to all the local places with a floorshow, I might be able to trace her. Naturally, a girl can't go into such places alone, so I asked Mr. Preston to act as my escort.'

You had to be there to hear the innocent ringing conviction of this new yarn of hers. Even Rourke didn't reject it out of hand.

'I see,' he said slowly. 'This friend now, what's her name?'

'Sally Dewes.'

'And you said you came here. Presumably you meant to Monkton City. Where are you from, Miss O'Hagan?'

'San Francisco,' she told him brightly.

He screwed up those wise old eyes.

'San Francisco. O'Hagan. I know a man up there by that name. Given name of Seamus. Wouldn't perhaps be a relative?'

'The only Seamus O'Hagan I know is my own father,' she replied solemnly.

'Can this be true?' he breathed. 'Is your father connected with the Brothers of Erin?'

'Master of the Lodge,' she nodded, sweetly. 'At least, he was last year.'

'Then you're Seamus O'Hagan's girl Abigail,' he almost shouted. 'Him and me are old buddies. We go way back. Here, girl, let me hold you by the hand.'

He jumped to his feet in excitement, grabbing at her extended fingers and pumping them up and down. It was obscene, the fuss he was making, but Abigail didn't seem to mind at all.

'You must come out to the house,' he announced. 'The missus'd never forgive me if I let any daughter of Seamus O'Hagan come to

142

the city without visiting. Say you'll come, now.'

One thing I had to admit about the vixen. She had the damndest skill in acquiring free meals.

'Why I'd love to, Captain. Perhaps I could call you later, and arrange a time?'

'Any time,' he boomed, 'any time at all. Wait'll I tell Annie. This is the best news in months. Now then, darling, tell me about your friend. This Sally Dewes. What are Missing Persons doing about her?'

'Well, I haven't actually bothered them,' she said, hesitantly. 'I don't know that she's really a missing person in the legal sense. This is more of a personal thing.'

If she'd been anyone else but good old Seamus O'Hagan's daughter, she'd have had a different reaction to that little speech. As it was, good old John Rourke simply gave her hand an extra pat.

'Personal, eh? Oh well, we won't enquire too much into that.' Then he turned to me, and some of the good humor left his face. Not all of it, because his delight was too genuine for him to change the mood entirely. 'As for your involvement here, I'm not going to say I'm entirely satisfied. But if you're helping Abigail look for her friend, just stick to that. Forget about the Prentice job. And one more thing. If you happen to hear where this Elizabeth Briggs is hiding herself, I'll expect you to call. And that I do mean.'

143

His eyes bored into me. I nodded.

'You got it, John, although I don't see why she should contact me.'

'Just the same,' he insisted.

'Will do. Er, could we go now?'

He would obviously have preferred for Abigail to leave her hand behind, but he released it finally. They stood there, exchanging fatuous remarks for a while, and then she walked with me to the door.

At the top of the stairs she said—

'Well, Stanley, that's another fine mess I got you out of.'

'You can save your charm for the Brothers of Erin,' I said, 'they seem to appreciate aspects of you that I don't see at all.'

We were halfway across the floor of the station-house when the street door revolved, disgorging the massive bulk of Detective Sergeant Gil Randall. I was all set to give him a muttered hallo and escape to the great outdoors, but he planted himself firmly in our path.

'Ah hah,' he greeted. 'The great detective. And am I finally going to meet someone from the fair City of Chattanooga?'

There was nothing sleepy about him as he stood there, drinking in Abigail. He gave more the impression of some huge predator, all set to pounce on this delectable morsel. Well, it wouldn't take long to put him in his place.

'This lady,' and I gave the word emphasis,

144

'is Miss Abigail O'Hagan from San Francisco. Her father is an old buddy of John Rourke's, and she just paid him a social visit.' Then I turned to the waiting lady. 'Let me introduce Detective Sergeant Randall, a member of Mr. Rourke's staff.'

'This is a pleasure,' she assured him, sticking out her hand. 'Mark has told me so much about you.'

Her hand disappeared inside one of those grab-cranes he keeps attached to the end of his arms.

'He has, huh? Well, he's kept very quiet about you, Miss O'Hagan. Scared of the competition, I imagine.'

You'd think it was love at first sight, the way they stood there. The girl was a positive menace. There ought to be something in the morality code to keep people like her away from the public.

'Yeah, well,' I mumbled, 'nice to see you Gil, but we have to be getting along. Busy evening.'

It was on the tip of my tongue to tell him that this dew-fresh specimen was an experimental feather-dancer in her spare time, but I held it back. As I was about to walk away, he said—

'Just a word, before you go. You'll excuse us, Miss O'Hagan? I won't keep him a minute.'

Grabbing me by the arm, he led me aside, and when he spoke, his voice was very low.

'I hope you're not getting a girl like this mixed up in whatever you're doing, because I have a newsflash for you.'

The retort I had ready in reply to the first part disappeared, when he said newsflash.

'What's going on?'

'I've just been round to ballistics, to find out why there's a delay on that gun used on your friend Briggs. Usual thing. It landed on the wrong desk, some guy who was off sick. But it's been processed now, or rather, the slugs have. We don't have the gun itself.'

'And?'

'And it's been used before, about a week ago. We have a Jane Doe on the slab, and there's no doubt the same gun was used in both cases. So, you look out for that little girl. This guy's already killed twice.'

I looked duly impressed, and for once it was not assumed.

'Good of you to tip me off, Gil.'

'Not you,' he contradicted, 'her. Rourke will skin everybody if anything should happen to her. Daughter of an old buddy, why that's like his own family.'

'I'll watch her,' I promised.

I didn't bother to explain the difficulties in trying to control Abigail H. O'Hagan the First. No one would have understood anyway.

After another brief session of beaming and bowing, I managed to get her out of that place, and parked in the front seat of the car.

'I don't know why you complain about those people,' she said peevishly. 'Perfectly lovely, all of them. And such gentlemen.'

I suppose it all depends on where you sit. In any case, I hadn't any time to argue with her.

'Randall just gave me some bad news,' I informed her. 'The gun that killed the man Briggs last night was also used to kill a woman last week. It only goes to underline what I told you about the danger here.'

She looked thoughtful.

'That's interesting. Who was the woman?'

'They don't know. She hasn't yet been identified. It's a Jane Doe case, and that means—'

'Please,' she interrupted. 'You're forgetting I'm a lawyer. I know what it means. We'd better go and take a look, huh?'

I was appalled.

'What for? If the police can't identify her, what chance would we have? And if you think I'm going to spend my evening poking around the City Morgue, you have another think coming.'

She fixed me with one of those looks.

'Now listen, Mark,' she began.

Ten minutes later, I found myself walking up the mortuary steps, still grumbling. I hate the place. It's always bitterly cold and damply sterile, with the stench of powerful chemical everywhere.

Inside, the night attendant was not pleased

147

about being disturbed from his duties. At that moment, these seemed to consist of drinking coffee and reading the afternoon race results.

'You got a permit?' he demanded.

I shook my head.

'This is a Jane Doe situation. There's no permit required in those cases. Anyone who thinks they might be able to identify the body is entitled to take a look.'

'Are you trying to tell me my job?' he said huffily.

'No, I'm not,' I assured him. 'I'm just suggesting you do it.'

He was getting ready to come back on that one, when Abigail decided to put in her two cents worth.

'Oh please, could we get this over with? That could be my dear sister in there, and I really don't think I can bear—'

To illustrate the point, she broke off, sniffling.

That had him up on his feet and moving. I nudged the sorrowing relative to tag along behind him. He led the way into that all-too-familiar high-ceilinged vault of a room, with the giant filing drawers lining each side. Striding briskly across, he grabbed a handle, and slid out one of the refrigerated compartments. Then he looked at me.

'You sure the lady is up to this?'

'I'm all right,' she replied for herself. 'Could we be quick, please?'

Nodding, he pulled back the sheet. We looked down at the unlined face of a woman who could have been anything between twenty and forty years old. Until that moment, it hadn't occurred to me to wonder where the wounds were. Seeing her now, I was grateful they hadn't been inflicted on the head.

Abigail gave a little gasp, and held on tight to my arm. The attendant looked at her enquiringly, and she shook her head.

'No,' she said, very quietly. 'No, that isn't her. Thank you.'

We left him there, and walked slowly out of the place. When we got outside, she took a deep breath of the evening air, and smiled tremulously.

'I'm sorry to make such a fuss. I really wasn't too concerned about going into that place, but it's the first time I've done it. I'm afraid the actual experience is rather more than I bargained for.'

'It's all right,' I assured her. 'Nobody enjoys it, but you were very insistent. Didn't gain much, did we?'

One more deep breath, and she was almost her old self. Now, she turned to me, with a mischievous smile.

'Oh, I don't know that I'd go that far. At least we can cross one person off our list now.'

'We could, if we knew who she was,' I agreed unhelpfully.

'Oh, didn't I tell you? Must have slipped my

mind. That dead woman in there is who I came here to find.'

At first I didn't take it in.

'Are you telling me that was—'

'Yes. The girl who started all this. That's Sally Dewes.'

## ELEVEN

'Sally Dewes? There's no doubt in your mind?'

We were seated in the nearest bar. The excuse was that Abigail needed a snort after her visit to the morgue. The fact was that I needed a place to sit and absorb this new information. Ice cubes rattled as she set down her glass.

'I really felt the need of that,' she announced. 'Doubt? How can there be any doubt? You either know someone or you don't, and I certainly know Sally Dewes. Knew, rather.'

The girl in the mortuary had been there almost a week. Five days, to be exact, because I checked the date on that drawer. And, if she was Sally Dewes, then a whole lot of thinking had to be scrapped, and new ideas set up in their place. The woman at the Maybelle Apartments, for a start. I had taken it for granted that she was Sally Dewes. She had denied it at first, but that I had expected. A

150

girl who's tied in with a large bundle of missing money wouldn't be too pleased about being tracked down. And, after we talked for a while, she had ceased to argue the point. At that time, I had assumed she felt there was no point in further denial. Now, knowing what I had just learned, I realised she had other reasons for letting me make my assumptions. One of those reasons, in fact the biggest reason, could easily be that she knew the unfortunate Sally was already dead. It's a simple rule of life that once someone finds what they're looking for, then they stop looking. If I thought Sally Dewes was alive, and living at 1622 Maybelle Apartments, then I would be unlikely to stumble across the fact of her death.

Point One.

It's also a simple rule of life that if the police have a body they can't identify, and some third party could identify if they chose, but they don't choose, then the afore-mentioned third party probably has some inside knowledge of how the body came to be deceased in the first place.

Point Two.

'You might at least talk to me,' grumbled Abigail.

I hesitated at first, then decided this was no time to be keeping her in the dark.

'This morning,' I said quietly, 'I was talking with Durrant's lady friend. I assumed she was Sally Dewes, and she let me go on thinking it.'

She was intrigued at once, and leant forward so she could catch every word.

'You didn't tell me that,' she accused.

'How could I? Every time I look for you, you're out waving your feathers at people. Anyway, you know now. This one I saw, she was acting as Durrant's assistant in his act, just a few months ago. They were working in some rat-trap called the Club Hotfoot.'

'Why, I know that place, it's back home,' she exclaimed.

'Right,' I confirmed. 'So where does that get us? Durrant and the girl, working in your town. At the same time, he was flexing his muscles with your friend Sally Dewes. Durrant is a number one attraction with the ladies—'

'—with some ladies,' she interposed, '—he's too fleshy to suit me—'

'—all right, with some ladies. Anyway, Sally Dewes certainly went for him. I haven't had time to shape this up properly; but let me try out some thinking on you. You could put up the woman's angle.'

'I'm all ears, professor,' she assured me gravely.

It was the kind of provocative remark she couldn't help making, to see what kind of reaction it would prompt, but I was not in the mood for games.

'Then pin 'em back,' I instructed. 'Our hero gets a few weeks work in another town. Being the way he is, he latches on to the local ladies, and one of them is Sally Dewes. At the same time, a man from Sally's place of work is breathing down her neck, a man who has access to company money. Let us suppose our hero sized up the situation. He wants his own place, like everybody else, but he can never raise the ante.'

'Like everybody else,' she agreed brightly.

'Don't interrupt. Now, he sees his chance. There's this girl, Sally Dewes, crazy about him. She'll do anything for him. Why shouldn't she be persuaded to get her man friend to steal from his company? Then, when they're both clear of the neighborhood, Durrant could come into the picture, relieve the guy of the money, and he and Sally could ride off into the sunset?'

I paused then, to let her know it was in order to bust in.

Abigail frowned, pulling at her lower lip while she thought. It was a nice lip.

'I don't know,' she said slowly. 'Joe McEvoy might be weak where Sally is concerned, but he's quite a man in other departments. He wouldn't just sit around quietly, and let Durrant rob him.'

Which led logically to another thought I was waiting to plant.

'Probably not. So it may have been necessary to kill McEvoy to get hold of the money.'

The reaction this time was much faster.

'That's out. For all kinds of reasons. First, and most important, is Sally herself. She's no better, no worse, than most women. I can understand quite easily how a woman would steal for a man. Cheat, lie for him if necessary. But murder is in an entirely different category. You'd have to find an unusual woman who will stand for that.'

'Maybe it wasn't put to her in those terms,' I objected. 'She probably thought they'd just disappear one night, while McEvoy was asleep.'

'Even if that were true, she would still react badly when she found out the truth.'

Abigail was so absorbed in her theoretical study of what Sally Dewes may or may not have agreed to, that she had forgotten one basic fact.

'You could be right,' I admitted. 'In fact, I would go so far as to say you're almost certainly right. And because of her objections, Sally Dewes is dead.'

She went pale then.

'That's right. Poor Sally. She may not have been my favorite person, but she didn't deserve that. But I still have an objection.'

'Then lodge it.'

Abigail nodded, marshalling her thoughts.

'I'm trying to get this together. I think it comes down to the gun. The reason we know of the connection between the murders of Briggs and Sally, is because the same gun was used. Your friend Sergeant Randall did not say the local mortuary was full of people killed with that gun. Just those two. So where is Joe McEvoy's body? Or are you going to suggest they used a different gun on him, and so the police haven't connected him with these other murders?'

I could see where Miss O'Hagan's lawyer training came in. She could think logically, when she wasn't busy aiming for that scatterbrain title. I shook my head.

'No, I don't think there would be another gun. It's very unusual to come across two weapons in this kind of case. If McEvoy is dead, and I'm coming firmly to believe that he is, there are several possibilities. First and foremost, the body may not yet have come to light. Second, he could have been killed some other way. Strangled, poisoned, knifed, the list is endless. And third, he could have been killed somewhere else. Right at the beginning, in fact. The moment he appeared with the money. He would be excited, jittery, an easy man to catch unawares by people he trusted.'

She spotted an objection to that at once.

'I doubt that last one. If he'd been killed in San Francisco, which is what you're suggesting, I would have known about it. The company would have known straight away.'

'Would they? Would anybody know who he was, including the police? San Francisco is a big city. Take away a man's identification, and

155

he's just another John Doe. You told me yourself, nobody reported McEvoy missing, so the police won't be looking out for him. That's a fine force they have up there, but they aren't clairvoyants.'

The tawny hair gleamed as she moved her head back and forth.

'All right, I concede the possibility. In any case, it's easy to check. All we do is to suggest to your police that they send the ballistic evidence to my police, and see if they're interested.'

Now she was thinking like a good little citizen. Trouble was, we were neither of us in that category, so far as this caper was concerned. We were up to our ears in concealed evidence, and the lawmen can get very tetchy about such details. I tried to explain this to her, and she listened, but with scant patience.

'Oh you,' she scoffed, when I was finished. 'You're a hell of a man for pointing out reasons why nobody should ever do anything. You know something? If the world was run by people like you, everybody would stay home all day. That way, they couldn't be involved in a street accident. In one month, the world would cease to exist, because everyone had died of starvation. But people can't do that. They have to get out there, where it's at. That's what we have to do, Preston. Not sit around on our butts. Well?'

'We have a place for people like you. It's just behind the City Library, and it's called Soapbox Alley. All the nuts get down there on Sunday mornings. Take your own box.'

'I'll be there Sunday,' she promised darkly. 'Meantime, there's the rest of the week to live through. What are we going to do?'

'First of all, let me tell you what we are not going to do. No wait—' as the objections registered immediately on her face—'hear me out. As of this moment, we are ahead of the game. No one else knows where we stand in all of this. Not the police, not Durrant and his lady friend, nobody. That gives us an edge. But we can lose it, if we start acting crazy. To anybody watching, we attract no attention. Agreed?'

She wasn't going to agree to anything so vague.

'That depends on what we're not going to do,' she said cautiously. 'If you mean we go home and lock the door, the answer is no.'

'Hear me out,' I repeated. 'Now, you first. Jack Durrant is expecting a cooch dancer tonight—'

'—don't you cooch me,' she snapped. 'This is a class specialty I'm putting on.'

'All right, then. He's expecting a class specialty.' Then, seeing the smug agreement on her face, I added. 'with feathers. At the moment, he doesn't connect you with anything outside the club. He expects a performer, and

157

I think you'd better go. Anything which upsets his routine is going to make him suspicious, and then he might do all kinds of unpredictable things. So long as he thinks he's safe, he'll stay put, and that's how we want him.'

Abigail had clearly been expecting me to warn her off the Bear-Bear Club, and made no bones about her relief at what I was now suggesting.

'Whew,' and she gave that locker-room snort of hers again, 'well, that keeps me in the action. What about you, coach?'

'I'm going to take a ride round to the Maybelle Apartments, have another chat with Durrant's girlfriend. Maybe I can scare her into some kind of admission.'

'You think it's likely? She didn't exactly tremble the last time you called, judging by what you told me.'

If I resented the implication that I was unlikely to frighten one defenseless female, I concealed it manfully.

'I wasn't talking about murder last time,' I pointed out smoothly. 'Once people hear that gas chamber being dropped into the conversation, it does wonders for their powers of communication.'

She lowered her eyes at me.

'I'll bet I could scare her better,' she claimed. 'One woman is always better at dealing with another one.'

'But that would mean I'd have to do your specialty,' I objected. 'You know your feathers would never fit me.'

That brought me one of her knowing grins.

'Love to see that,' she claimed. 'Well, O.K., we'll do it your way. Just wait a few minutes, while I powder my nose.'

She seemed to be away a long time, but then, they always are.

Finally she came back, all smiles.

'Let's get on with it,' she suggested. 'I imagine I'm taking a cab out to the club, right? But first I have to go back for my costume.'

It was almost an hour later when I packed her into a cab, and watched it pull away into traffic. She turned and waved at me through the rear window, and I hoped I wasn't taking too much of a chance, with what was rapidly becoming her precious safety.

A little after nine thirty I parked outside the Maybelle Apartments. This time I knew my way around, and was soon leaning on the buzzer at No. Sixteen Twenty-Two.

'Bill collector?'

A voice from behind made me spin round. An elderly man in a blue coverall stood watching me.

'Why would I be a bill collector?' I queried. 'And who are you?'

'Who I am is the janitor here, that's who,' he replied tersely. 'And the way the lady took off, it wouldn't surprise me none if you was a bill collector. Or worse.'

From the way he was sizing me up, it was obvious that worse would fit the case better.

'Took off? You mean she's moved away?'

'Seems likely,' he confirmed. 'Leastways, she cleaned the place out, and give me the keys. I guess that's moving out, all right. And you still didn't say who you was.'

'I am Deputy Sheriff Preston,' I told him crisply, 'and I am here on a police matter. I want this woman's forwarding address, and fast.'

Inquisitive was replaced by fear now.

'I don't know nothing,' he whined. 'People come, people go. I ain't employed here to spy on folks.'

'Never mind that, what about the address?'

'Didn't leave one. Not with me. Just went. You wanta check inside?'

He was already reaching at his waist, where a large circular bunch of keys was dangling.

'All right. Open it up.'

He nodded anxiously, and spidery fingers inserted a key in the lock. I went in first, and there was no doubt my bird had flown. The place was thoroughly depersonalised, as only deserted living quarters can be. The bathroom yielded a scrap of dried soap and a crumpled toothpaste tube. In the kitchen, a torn and soiled cloth lay on the drainer. A tattered mattress lay naked in the bedroom, an empty Kleenex box on the floor beside it.

'She didn't leave much, huh?' I grunted.

'Not a damned thing,' assented my companion.

We turned back into the living area, where the only sign of recent human occupation was the overflowing waste basket. Well, it was all I had. I knelt down beside it, and began to root through.

'What're you going to find in there?'

This from over my crouching shoulder.

'Who knows? Old letters. Anything that might give me a lead.'

I was almost at bottom when I found the torn wrapper. It was just a narrow band of paper, with an imprint on it. The imprint was that of a San Francisco bank, and its original role in life had been to go around a bundle of crisp new folding money. This had to have been part of the money stolen by Joseph P. McEvoy, and it was all the confirmation I needed that time was short.

I stuffed the paper in my pocket, and straightened up.

'What's that you took?'

'Evidence. Now, think carefully. What time was it when this woman handed in her keys?'

'I was watching the Bristol program,' he said, without hesitation. 'That comes on at eight o'clock. So, it was eight fifteen, eight twenty.'

She had well over an hour's start on me. By now, she could be anywhere, but there was

161

only one place I cared about. That was the place where a certain feather dancer would be making her debut this same night. Mumbling some nonsense about formal statements to the puzzled janitor, I got out of there fast, and headed for the car.

Fortunately there was no police officer on my route out to the Bear-Bear Club, or I should have collected a speeding ticket without fail. When I screeched into the crowded forecourt, I sighed with relief, and climbed out. It was now ten twenty, and Abigail would be due onstage at any time from then on. I had already checked the thirty-eight before calling on the woman who was not Sally Dewes, and was glad of the hard comfort against my middle as I walked towards the club entrance. Two people were dead already, with McEvoy a possible third. The answer to it all was somewhere inside that lighted building, and I know from experience that once someone gets over the hurdle of that first murder, the process comes easier.

Business was good tonight, about two-thirds capacity, and I stood at the bar, cradling a scotch on the rocks, and searching the faces of the diners. It wasn't an easy task, what with heads bobbing up and down, and waiters passing to and fro the whole time, but after ten minutes I was satisfied there was no one in the audience who was involved. Not that I was aware of, I amended.

The background music came suddenly to an end, and the smiling figure of Jack Durrant walked out on to the desktop dance floor. He went into his warmup, and they liked him. It was hard to relate the confident, relaxed man with the still figure I'd left behind in the mortuary, but the connection was there, and now I could prove it. Before I could do anything, I wanted Abigail out of the way. The best place for her was out in the plain view of the customers, and I was impatient for her to begin her act.

'And tonight, for the first time in Monkton City, the Bear-Bear Club is proud to bring you a rare treat. No less than one of San Francisco's top attractions, the gorgeous, the scrumptious, the delectable—' he stopped for a second, looking behind him, '—sorry to keep you in suspense folks, but before I let this girl onto the stage, I have to check the boys in the band are strapped down. Yes, they are. And now, for the first time ever, we proudly present—Sugar Plum La Chatte.'

The lights blacked out. Then a single beam hit the curtains at the side, and at the same time the drummer faked a gunshot. There was a gasp from the audience, the men anyway, and there was Abigail. There weren't quite as many feathers as I'd been led to believe, but no one complained about the shortage. Any gap in the feathers was filled with Abigail, and I didn't hear anybody ask for his money back.

Her spot would occupy the next few minutes, and that was the break I needed to take a look around backstage. The place was still in semi-darkness, and there was no one to take any interest in one fully-clothed male slipping through the gloom. The narrow passageway at the side was deserted, and that struck me as odd. I would have thought a big ladies' man like Durrant would want to catch an eyeful of the moulting process. I moved quietly along to the door of the room where I'd found him on my last visit. There was the sound of voices on the other side. Easing the gun into my side pocket, I turned the handle and stepped in.

Durrant's lady friend was in full flight, calling him every name under the sun. He stood a few feet in front of her, a helpless expression on his face. At the sound of my entrance, they both looked round.

'What the hell do you want?' snarled Durrant. 'I told you to keep away from here.'

'I told you he'd cause trouble, but you wouldn't listen,' contributed the woman.

'You were right, lady,' I confirmed. 'I'm trouble, all right, and I'm here. Seems there's a couple of murders need to be explained. You've got the job.'

She looked quickly at the man.

'Now it's two murders. This morning he said one, and that was bad enough. You said you never heard of this Briggs.' She turned to me.

'Who else got killed that we don't know?'

'Don't listen to him, Angie,' barked Durrant. 'I told you, he's just a guy out looking for a fast buck. A trouble-maker.'

'You told me,' she sneered. 'Is that right? Well, it was you told me we only tricked that dumb broad Dewes out of twenty thousand. According to this man, it should have been thirty-eight thousand. I know, you, Jack. You kind of forgot to mention the rest of the money, because you wanted to keep it all yourself.'

'Shut up, before you get us both in a lot of trouble,' hissed Durrant.

I laughed sourly.

'How much more trouble do you need?' I asked. 'The bodies are piling up all over town. As for that dumb broad, Angie, she's lying down at the city morgue, full of bullet holes. She was killed by the same gun as killed Briggs today. You don't suppose old Jack's been keeping little secrets from you, do you?'

'Now Angie—' he began.

'Now nothing.'

She flipped open the black leather purse on her arm and dived a hand inside. When it came out, her fist was lost behind a gray Army revolver. Durrant nodded.

'Good girl, hand that over.'

Her fist did not move.

'What for? So you can kill him? Me too, maybe? You've got nothing to lose now, Jack.

165

And you've still got all that extra money somewhere. You could be in Mexico in an hour.'

I didn't like the set whiteness of her face. It was the look of someone getting ready to squeeze a trigger.

'Take it easy, Angie,' I said quietly. 'I can probably fix it so you're kept out of this.'

'You don't know Jack Durrant,' she informed me through tight lips. 'You think he'll take a rap alone, if he thinks he can drag me into it? Just shut up, both of you, I'm thinking.'

From the club came a roar of applause. We stood there, in a frozen tableau, waiting for Angie's next move. Behind me, the door flew open.

'Hey,' squealed Abigail excitedly, then 'oh.'

Angie had turned automatically at the interruption. Durrant flung himself at the gun, but he was still a foot away from it, when it exploded with an almighty roar. He gave a bellow of pain, and dived to the floor. I stepped quickly in front of Abigail. Angie swung the gun towards me uncertainly.

'Calm down,' I urged her. 'All right, so you've shot Durrant. He attacked you, and I'll be a witness to that. But shoot me, shoot her, and you're just an animal. You'll be a kill-on-sight poster.'

She bit her lip, nodding.

'You just saved your life. You know why?'

I didn't care why, so long as she wasn't going to shoot. The thing was to keep her talking.

'Because you're a smart girl?' I hazarded. 'Because you know I'm talking sense?'

'No,' she negatived. 'Because of the way you got between me and that Sugar Plum. She's no stranger to you, I guess. You know what he'd have done?' She nodded grimly at the prostrate Durrant. 'He'd have held me in front of him as a shield. Now, stay lucky, and keep out of my way. I'm going out of here.'

She edged around us towards the door, the revolver very steady in her grip. Reaching behind me for Abigail's hand, I pulled her round with me, as Angie backed out.

The massive figure of Randall suddenly blocked the open doorway.

'What in hell is going on here?' he bellowed, at Angie's back.

She swung around. There was a sudden rush of bare legs, perfume and feathers, as Abigail flew horizontally past me. Her legs scissored around Angie's gun arm, and they both crashed to the floor, the revolver slithering uselessly into a corner.

Angie sat up at once, cursing, as her broken arm dangled. The feathered fury bounced to her feet, dusting herself off.

'Never done that dive before, only at practise,' she informed me, with a beaming smile.

167

'What was that, some kind of karate?' I asked, bewildered.

'Kung Fu,' she corrected. 'You're going to have to get up to date you know, Mark.'

'All right,' said Randall patiently. 'I asked you once. I'll ask you again. What the hell is going on?'

Durrant stirred and sat up, clutching a ruined shoulder.

'It's a long story, Gil,' I replied. 'Maybe Miss O'Hagan and I better come down to headquarters and fill in some of the details.'

'All the details,' he corrected. 'Who's that guy, for a start?'

'That's Jack Durrant. He almost certainly killed Bosun Briggs, and that is probably the weapon he used.'

'Uh huh. And where does this one fit in?'

He indicated the weeping Angie, now past caring.

'I'm not sure,' I admitted. 'Maybe not at all. But she can certainly fill in some of the spaces. Tell me Gil, what made you come out here?'

Those heavy-lidded eyes flicked back and forth from Abigail to me.

'Seems we got this anonymous telephone call. We ought to put the ballistics picture on the wire to the San Francisco P.D. See if they had anything like it. They did. They have a white male Caucasian John Doe up there. About forty-five years old. Been dead about a week. Does it suggest anything?'

168

Now we knew what had happened to Joseph P. McEvoy.

'Not right off,' I denied.

'Nor to me,' chipped in Abigail sweetly.

But there are times when Detective Sergeant Randall doesn't take sugar.

'It was a woman made the call,' he growled. 'She also suggested that the gun might be found out here at the club tonight.'

'Some women are awful on the phone aren't they?' she asked conversationally. 'They just chatter away. Wonder who it was?'

'Yeah, I wonder.' He bent down, to help Angie to her feet. 'I've got some help outside. We'll get these birds down to headquarters. I suggest you follow, and I mean now. C'm on, you.'

This to Durrant, who stumbled past and out, without a word. Randall and Angie followed him.

'I guess it's all over, h'm?'

Abigail put her hands on her hips and looked at me. There was nothing else on her hips, just hands.

'I guess it is,' I agreed.

'And you didn't even catch my act,' she grumbled.

'I'm catching the finale now,' I corrected.

She only had four feathers left. And one of those was on her head.

'It's better with the music,' she complained.

'I doubt it. You'd better get some more

clothes on.'

That brought me a pout.

'I'll bet you're the only man on earth who would say that. Most men give me trouble in the opposite direction.'

'I'll bet,' I grinned, and kissed her lightly on the lips. 'Let's understand each other, Miss O'Hagan. First, you are going to get dressed. Second, we are going to police headquarters, to get ourselves straightened out with the law.'

'Sounds exciting, I must say,' she returned, in a bored voice. 'How about third?'

'Third,' I counted off my middle finger, 'I'm going to give you plenty of trouble in that opposite direction.'

She shivered all over, making the feathers jiggle disastrously.

'Is that a promise?'

'Think of it more as a threat.'

'Oh, goodie.'